Haghdar

The Great

Story

A Fiction

STEVEN HAMIDI

Copyright © 2018 Steven Hamidi
All rights reserved. Each copy of this book is licensed for the enjoyment of the buyer only. It may not be re-sold or given away to other people. If you would like to share this book with another individual, please purchase another copy (or copies) for each recipient. Thank you for your consideration. This book or any part of it, individually or cumulatively, may not be reproduced or redistributed in any form or manner, stored in any retrieval system or transmitted electronically or otherwise by any means whether visual or audio, without written consent of the author, except as provided by the copyright laws of the United States of America.
First Edition

PAGE PUBLISHING, INC.
New York, NY

First originally published by Page Publishing, Inc. 2018

For licensing or permission please contact:
stevehamidi314@yahoo.com

Haghdar The Great Story is a work of **fiction**. Names, characters, businesses, places, events, locales, and incidents are either the products of the author's imagination or used in a fictitious manner. Any resemblance to actual or fictitious persons, living or dead, actual or fictitious places, or actual or fictitious events is purely and entirely coincidental.

ISBN 978-1-64298-399-9 (Paperback)
ISBN 978-1-64462-791-4 (Hardcover)
ISBN 978-1-64298-400-2 (Digital)

Printed in the United States of America

CONTENTS

Chapter 1 - Land of Mystery 7
Chapter 2 - The Fight 12
Chapter 3 - Justice for All 16
Chapter 4 - Wealth 23
Chapter 5 - Imperfection 28
Chapter 6 - Skies Help 34
Chapter 7 - Return to Civilization 38
Chapter 8 - Hero 44
Chapter 9 - Rise of Toufan 50
Chapter 10 - Enemy Counseling 53
Chapter 11 - Interim Defeat 56
Chapter 12 - The Reception 60
Chapter 13 - Magician 63
Chapter 14 - Farewell 68
Chapter 15 - The Battle 72
Chapter 16 - The Meeting 78
Chapter 17 - Joy to All 84
Chapter 18 - The Departure 89
Chapter 19 - The Scheme 97
Chapter 20 - Lies that Fly 102
Chapter 21 - The Escape 106
Chapter 22 - Oh, Boy 111
Chapter 23 - Life after Death 121
Chapter 24 - Calm Before the Storm 131
Chapter 25 - Surviving Catastrophe 135
Chapter 26 - Action 147

Chapter 27 - Arrested	152
Chapter 28 - The Punishment	156
Chapter 29 - The Climb	161
Chapter 30 - The Winner	168
Chapter 31 - Succession	174
Chapter 32 - No Conflict	180
Chapter 33 - Journey	187
Chapter 34 - Homeland	191
Chapter 35 - Shake Up	197
Chapter 36 - First Cut	203
Chapter 37 - The News	207
Chapter 38 - The Decision	212
Chapter 39 - Preparation	220
Chapter 40 - First Battle	225
Chapter 41 - The Arrangements	229
Chapter 42 - The War	236
Chapter 43 - Final Decision	244
Chapter 44 - Finale	249
About the Author	259

CHAPTER ONE

LAND OF MYSTERY

Thousands of light-years apart in a universe parallel to ours on a planet in the fifth dimension, there lived a king who ruled over a small but wealthy country called Mantik (meaning "logic"). Mantik was at the foot of a range of mountains, including the tallest one known to man, and enjoyed affluence of water, good land, and farming riches. Mantik had a small yet brave army comprised of well-trained soldiers who had protected her against invaders and other hostile foreign warriors for hundreds of years. Mantik was accessible only from the west and south since it was surrounded by tall and practically impossible to pass mountains to the north and most of the east. The security, the affluence of natural resources, and the wisdom of Mantik's king made it the envy of many kings who aspired to conquer it but could not afford to.

The king of Mantik had three young and brave sons who learned from the wisdom of their father and his court ministers. There also were certain high priests who brought strong belief to the country, the royalty, and the courtyard. The priests served the people and the king of Mantik well.

Mantik was east of a very powerful, wealthy, and widespread country called Fars (meaning "distances"). The king and people of Mantik were on the assumption that Fars extended to the end of the known world, where there was nothing beyond the Fars kingdom since no one from Mantik ever traveled past Fars and came back. Fars presumably ended at the edge of the planet.

Mantik paid reasonable taxes annually to the king of Fars. Those taxes were nominal compared with the wealth of Mantik and the amounts similar countries paid to Fars, but none of the countries complained about it. Both countries avoided conflict since any dispute—or even worse, a war—could cost them dearly. The two countries paid mutual respect to one another for as long as memory allowed.

The king of Mantik was just to his people yet an ambitious man who always dreamt of defeating and hence ruling Fars and therefore the world, but did not have the power or the wisdom to achieve it.

The king of Mantik frequently shared with his top generals and especially his three sons and high priests, his vision of conquering Fars and thereby ruling the known world. Top generals and, in particular, high priests advised him every time to avoid his ambitions as many kings fell to their graves carrying the vision of overtaking Fars. They told him the people of Mantik had good life, one which was the envy of many nations. They reiterated Fars was fair to Mantik, and the taxes they paid did not diminish the quality of life of the people of Mantik. Further, Fars practically protected Mantik since any army wishing to attack Mantik from the west had to go through Fars, which had been impossible for centuries. They told him Fars and Mantik were allies, and in fact, Fars warranted Mantik's security and sovereignty for the reason that no power could match that of the Fars empire and thereupon did not dare to attack or occupy Fars's neighboring ally. Upon the king's continuous insistence, high priests told him that according to the myths, there existed a powerful and mystic bird named Seepar (meaning "shield") living on top of the highest mountain to the north of Mantik and that whoever could kill the monstrous bird and washed his body in its blood would be able to defeat and conquer Fars and thereafter rule the world. They warned him many men had taken the journey to Seepar's nest, but none ever came back. Seepar had lived for thousands of years, and many brave men disappeared to its account. The myth said Seepar would suck all the air around whoever approached it, suffocate them, and then consume them. Every time Seepar ate a brave young man, it absorbed his strength and youth, therefore becoming younger and stronger. The myth also said it was the good luck of Seepar that brought health, wealth, and happiness to Mantik; hence, once it were killed, the Mantik kingdom would turn to ruins, and its people would perish in sickness and poverty.

The king, however, had a greater vision than Mantik's fortune and was preparing himself for the big move. He studied thousands of years of myths about Seepar, what made it strong, and what could possibly make it weak.

The king of Mantik had put himself and his three sons through extensive training, both physically and spiritually, until his youngest son was fifteen years old. He believed it was time to bring the fight to Seepar, to kill it and then wash himself and hopefully his sons in its blood as it was prerequisite to taking the war to the Fars. The king thought it was now or never and better now than never. He first inquired his sons' opinion to take on such a dangerous yet rewarding venture. The young lads, being ambitious themselves, also believed this was their time as their father, the king, was not getting any younger, and they undeniably needed his wisdom and strength if they had any chance to kill Seepar. The thought of defeating Fars and subsequently ruling the known world lifted their spirit, hence insured the king of their commitment to this morally and philosophically high prophecy—one worthy of their lives in case they had to sacrifice it as young and promising as they were.

Thereafter, the king of Mantik discussed his plan with the high priests and promised them that upon his return, which meant he had already killed Seepar, he would conquer Fars and migrate his people there, where they did not need the good luck and fortune of Seepar. The priests quarreled against the king's intentions. They made the argument that the king should not throw away the good life of his, of his sons, and of Mantik's people in search of what was only a myth and, if it existed, extremely dangerous to all, and more importantly possibly ending the thousands of years of comfortable living of the people of Mantik. They contended that such an unimpressive expedition might not be justified by any cause at any level. Their advice was to forget it and instead rule the country as his ancestors had done for hundreds of years.

However, the king and his sons were determined to take up the task and to start their trek immediately and without further delay.

"The decision is made," the king proclaimed, "and now we must plan for the future." The king continued, "a secured future filled with glory and happiness for the entire mankind, including but not limited to those of Mantik and Fars, to coexist side by side as one nation, one idea, one life full of joy afforded by the sacrifices of the king and his sons. That humane purpose of the scheme must be the essence of the king's duty, and the prospect of danger did not and neither should prevent the king from attaining it. Those are the fundamentals that differentiate the king from his subjects even though not agreed upon or understood by the common citizens."

The fierce accent of the king and the depiction of his high morals silenced the priests. They dropped their heads in admiration and recognition of his resolve.

The king of Mantik assigned the governance of his country to a council consisting of high priests, court administrators, and his bravest and most trusted generals.

And so, the king's journey with his three sons began. According to the myth, it would take two years to climb to the top of the highest mountain where Seepar was said to have lived.

CHAPTER TWO

The Fight

The king of Mantik took with him the strongest and biggest mules available in his country to carry heavy weaponry needed to fight Seepar. The mules also carried supplies for the king and his three sons during their journey to the top of the highest mountain, where Seepar was said to be nesting.

The king decided to travel fast at the lower grounds and, once arriving at the higher levels, proceed with caution because Seepar might patrol there for food and possible risk takers. As they used their supplies, they kept the mules as spare or, better yet, to feed Seepar with them. It was said in the myths that first, once Seepar was full, it could not consume more food, and second, mule feed would make Seepar slow and slightly confused. They needed every chance they could put their hands on.

They realized, as they climbed higher, the climate got colder, and there was less air to breathe. Thus, they knew they were getting closer to the top of the mountain, where Seepar was said to have lived for thousands of years. At some point, before they reached on top of the highest mountain, inside a cave where they made sure there was no trace of Seepar, they assembled for the last time before the confrontation to review their fight blueprint. From there they were able to have a view of the peak of the top mountain from afar. It appeared there was a huge flat rock, more like an extensive sacrificial deck on top of a long vertical solid-rock pillar backed by a steep cliff on top of the highest mountain, which one could reach only by either air or creeping under the bedrock and moving horizontally under it to arrive at the edge and then climbing over. Both accesses were impossible to pass. They could not fly, and the gravity would prevent them from crawling under the bedrock horizontally. Worse, Seepar could hear or smell them and attack when they were in the most difficult position—apparently suicide. The king referred to one of the old myths; he told his children they could not get to the top of the bedrock alive and therefore must force Seepar to bring the fight to them. His sons asked how they could force Seepar to come to them other than when it was sure it could consume them. Seepar knew it was safe on top of the bedrock. Most likely that was the reason it lived there. The king replied they must set a trap by presenting his youngest son, who also was the strongest and bravest, as bait to seemingly prove their loyalty and appreciation for the fortune and good luck Seepar had brought to Mantik.

The king told his sons there was a high probability that any of them—and if they were careless, all of them—could be killed by Seepar; thus, it was appropriate to perform traditional rituals before they proceeded farther. It was difficult, especially for the king, to perform rituals at the face of almost certain death looming upon his children and himself. Nonetheless, he conducted the ritual with resolve. There was no turning back at this point of their excursion.

With a heavy heart and tears in his eyes, the king then put his youngest son on the back of a mule and tied his hands and legs together under the mule's belly to prove to Seepar from afar that he was truly a sacrifice. However, he made the ties in a manner that his son could untie easily by one special move only the high priests knew and taught him. The king also left in his son's hand a dagger infected by the deadliest poison the priests of Mantik could provide with which his son was to stab Seepar. He then showed his son how to release the ties fast and fight Seepar once it came down to consume him.

They climbed to the foot of the vertical elevation on top of the mountain and called on Seepar. The king and his two sons performed rituals of respect and admiration and bowed to the powers of Seepar. To their surprise, Seepar appeared from behind the bedrock on top of the high cliff, the bottom of which was said in the myths to have been the deepest parts of the dark world. Seepar was huge with a fierce appearance. They had never seen such a monstrous façade. Fear pierced through their hearts and souls. Seepar looked down on them as no man had reached this far for hundred years. Because no man had come in such a long time, Seepar was hungry and relatively weak. It needed to feast on the young and strong man quickly to rejuvenate its powers.

The king shouted, as loud as he could, "Your Majesty, we have brought a sacrifice since we know no man has come before your greatness for hundred years, and you need your strength. Mantik owes its wealth and good fortune to your graciousness, and it is said that without you, this fortune would disappear, and the people of Mantik would perish in disgrace and despair. Herewith in order to prove our loyalty and appreciation, we have brought this sacrifice for you and will leave this place so you may enjoy him in peace." Then the king and his other two sons left the young man there and, at one opportune moment, crept under the bedrock where Seepar could not see them.

Seepar waited a long time to make sure they were gone but needed to feast on the young in order to regain its strength and powers and therefore cautiously flew to the young man. As Seepar sat atop of a rock close enough to consume the king's son, he freed his hands and, with the dagger, struck upon Seepar. At the same time, the king and his other two sons rushed out from under the bedrock and ran toward Seepar to kill it. The strike of the king's youngest son's dagger hit the top of a fingernail of Seepar and cut a very small piece of it. The king and his other sons joined him, and a ferocious fight began. The king reached for Seepar's broken fingernail and collected it. The fight took hours, and Seepar killed the king's sons one by one and severely injured the king. Seepar, not having eaten in hundred years, had used all its strength fighting four strong men and hence started to eat them to regain its powers. The king recognized Seepar was gaining back its strength and powers. He was fearful for his own life and therefore took advantage of the opportunity, and while Seepar was consuming his sons, he escaped the place downward toward Mantik.

CHAPTER THREE

JUSTICE FOR ALL

The king of Fars was a wise and generous man, a master of politics and warfare who championed freedom, justice, happiness, and wealth accumulation throughout his empire. He believed in the freedom of man and encouraged his people to follow through with their dreams. He made every effort to provide the necessary grounds to afford all citizens an equitable chance to achieve their goals. The kingdom offered good education, jobs, and opportunities for innovation.

Social classes in Fars consisted of three major categories—military personnel, merchants, and servants of the executive branch, including the ministers. The militants held the highest level among the three social classes. Many young individuals' ideal was to join the armed forces and climb the ranks. Generals were highly respected and wealthy. Top generals were made kings of territories and regions. The king of Fars was called the king of the kings.

Citizens of Fars were entitled to own slaves, who were mostly prisoners of wars. However, once they proved loyalty to their masters, they were treated relatively fairly. Contrary to the rest of the world, including but not limited to Mantik, slaves had certain basic rights in Fars. They might not be punished excessively or abused. For high crimes subject to severe punishment, slaves were allowed to be heard by a special panel, and the ruling of the panel was final. The owners were allowed to free slaves, which they often did once proven they could peacefully live and blend in a civilized society and did not raise arms against Fars or commit treason. Children of slaves were born as slaves but had more rights, such as access to limited education and better nutrition and shelter. Most slaves freed were the second generation. Many of them stayed with their masters as free employees entitled to benefits all other employees enjoyed.

The king did not own any slave personally and was not in favor of keeping slaves, but the issue was controversial. On one hand, he did not believe in the "no prisoner" motto chanted by some generals. Keeping the captivated enemies in prison was expensive and required extensive infrastructure and resources. On the other hand, some slave owners were not in favor of freeing them prematurely; among other reasons, they provided workforce for simple tasks. These slave owners served Fars well and were comparatively lenient toward the slaves. Many of them freed slaves after few years. Nonetheless, the king desired to find a solution to end slavery, and his ultimate goal was to establish a nation where there existed only free men.

The king of kings made sure his just laws and their respective spirits were enforced equitably throughout the country and the wealth of the empire utilized as best as possible to provide underlying fundamentals and security for citizens to develop and follow their ways of a good life. He encouraged and welcomed varied ethnicities, religions, and races. He was good to his people yet had a firm hand with enemies and did not allow them, be it outside his country or within, to avert, delay, or derail his programs of development and progress. At a younger age, he personally brutally punished or executed some rivals sworn to disrupt his plans. He was merciful to all but those agents of the gods of darkness who were against him and his ideals.

The king of Fars was a warrior himself who had led his army to many victories. His mere appearance in the battlefield cast the darkness of fear and submission onto the heart and soul of many adversaries.

The militants of Fars kingdom were brave and conquered many countries. A special division of the armed forces enforced laws and maintained order and fought crime and corruption based on the governing laws, rules, and regulations. The king personally trained and educated his top generals to be kind and merciful to the people of the countries they conquered and to grant asylum to soldiers and warriors of those countries if they simply promised to be loyal to the king. Nonetheless, he did not tolerate those who turned back on their promise, especially if they raised arms against Fars again. Their punishment was severe, mainly execution.

He specifically instructed his army to respect the freedom of the people of those countries they conquered and to allow them to live their way of life as long as they did not raise arms against Fars or did not commit treason. He punished any of his militants or administrators who broke the laws regarding the liberty and rights of the people of those countries.

People from other countries ruled by dictators sent invitations to the king of Fars to conquer their countries and free them from ruthless rulers and their executioners. They opened their castles' and hearts' doors and welcomed the king of Fars.

The Fars kingdom spread to the west, beyond where an ordinary man could imagine. To the east, Fars was bordered by Mantik. Most of these countries, including Mantik, were independent in their conduct of internal and external affairs as long as they were united with Fars, paid their reasonable taxes, and sent warriors to help Fars in case they were summoned.

To the west of Fars, it was believed there was no land worth fighting for, and therefore, small rulers existed who paid taxes to Fars. Many of the young and brave soldiers from those regions voluntarily joined the Fars armed forces in an effort to achieve high ranks there. The most powerful country to the west of Fars was called Toufan (meaning "storm").

High-ranking generals in the Fars kingdom enjoyed more of the better things in life, ruled territories and regions, and were kings themselves. The king of kings was expansively generous to them and reflected on them to rule their countries in the same manner he governed them.

The kings subject of the king of kings, nevertheless, would, from time to time, visit neighboring countries such as Mantik and Toufan, depending on which one was within reach, to collect small amounts of additional taxes, the best of warriors, horses, and beautiful young women for their extra pleasure. The king of Fars knew about these activities but did not interfere directly since they kept these countries quiet and orderly, and those immaterial takings did not create big waves of dissatisfaction; however, he did not approve of them either. He often implicitly advised these generals to stop their activities, which otherwise could give rise to the citizens' dissatisfaction.

Many of these small rulers outside the Fars kingdom fought among themselves for food, land, and wealth, which kept them at the surviving level, except Mantik to the east, which was secured by mountains and brave soldiers, and Toufan to the west. Toufan's women were generally beautiful, patriotic, and ambitious. Toufan women never left their country by will and expected their men to be brave warriors and not only defenders of Toufan but also conquerors of other lands. They believed a man was to work on land, protect land, or conquer it. The love of land and, above all, Toufan, was superior to any love or loyalty for Toufan's women.

The king of Toufan was a wise and ambitious warrior who, in order to achieve his dream of conquering Fars, quietly but consistently defeated weaker rulers, enclosed their lands to his, and drafted their soldiers, only to create his own small empire.

The king of Toufan was confronted with his countrymen's contempt, who voiced their complaints for losing their sons and daughters and, equally important, the best of their horses to Fars generals. Further, Toufan did not enjoy many natural resources known to man, and Fars taxes were an imposition to the quality of the lives of the people of Toufan. As the time passed and Toufan added more and more of the smaller nations to its country and unified them under its flag, the confidence of the people and especially the generals rose, and therefore they demanded from their king to adopt a firm position and take stricter measures against Fars generals in order to prevent them from violating Toufan's laws. Specifically, they insisted that the taking of the young and horses must stop.

The king of Fars knew about the rise of Toufan, but his spies and the intelligence they provided consistently reported to him that the Fars armed forces could defeat and conquer Toufan's kingdom within hours if he decided to do so. The king of Fars did not wish to involve his military in less worthy wars, which could deteriorate the military personnel's highly trained physical and mental abilities; hence, he preferred one ruler to do the job for him and kept all these smaller rulers in order. As in any fight, the king knew there always was a chance for opponents, large or small, to achieve victory because of unknown and surprising factors. He realized early in his life that no matter how accurately and profoundly the war plans and strategies were drawn, the element of surprise might not be eliminated nor underestimated.

The generals of the Fars empire ruling western regions neighboring Toufan continued to frequently attack these adjacent territories and especially Toufan to collect additional taxes, beautiful women, young soldiers, and particularly horses, as the only thing besides beautiful women worth their effort to fight the west was the best of the breed of horses. The horses outside the west border of Fars kingdom and especially in Toufan were said to be the best in the world.

These countries, mainly those next to Fars headed by Toufan, were dissatisfied with the Fars generals' activities and hence had sent messages to the king of kings requesting to stop them. They claimed they regularly paid their taxes and therefore must be subject to the king of kings' protection, that such activities were widespread, reduced his popularity, and might even cause revolt and disobedience to his just governance. The king of kings continued his policy of softly deliberating with his generals about the complainants in order to keep the fire under the ashes or possibly extinguish it.

The Fars kingdom taxed Toufan based on the same rules and calculations that were applied to all other countries the king of Fars taxed equitably. But the impact of the taxes was severe on Toufan because of the lack of sufficient natural resources. Moreover, Toufan's women, who were independent in nature and, more importantly, did not wish to be forced to ever leave their beloved land, constantly complained to their husbands, brothers, and fathers, including generals, and therefore added to the pressure.

Fars generals went to Mantik mostly for its wealth and to collect extra taxes since women to the east commonly were not as beautiful and cultured as the ones in the west. Mantik's women mostly preferred to stay at home and did not participate much in social and political affairs. They were dependent on their men and preferred a lavish lifestyle. They almost never worked on the land; however, they raised wise and brave sons who protected the country and accumulated wealth. Mantik did not have many horses either because of its mountainous environment but had the best of mules, which could climb mountains with ease at a much faster pace without many casualties.

CHAPTER FOUR

WEALTH

The king of Fars, during absence of the king of Mantik, received reports that Mantik was in chaos. Her king and his heirs went to follow a myth and did not come back for years; its people, lacking order, rioted and killed many of the members of the high council appointed by the king before his departure. Mantik had lost not only its fortunes to ruins but also many brave soldiers to either addiction or getting killed in wars against other rulers in that part of the world who wanted to take advantage of Mantik's weak and unstable situation. Mantik, in addition to being on her way to complete destruction, was becoming a danger to the Fars empire since many of the other smaller rulers also rioted seemingly against each other but secretly formed forces against Fars. They refused to pay taxes, paid late, or paid less than what was allotted to them. Instead they used the wealth of Mantik to equip themselves with better weapons and military gear, conducting intense training and hiring mercenaries. Their strength was growing fast, and that gave them a reasonable basis to convince many other rulers to join them in preparation for the ultimate war against Fars. These rulers had heard that to the west of Fars, some countries led by Toufan were arising and strengthening their military capabilities for an opportune moment to attack Fars and not only put an end to the generals' visits but also break the Fars empire into pieces and share its wealth and power. They sent messengers to Toufan to express their dissatisfaction with the Fars generals' activities and especially the king since he did not take any action to stop them and, in effect, allowed them to continue their misbehavior. The king of Toufan sent messages back to the east to confer upon his dissatisfaction and that there must be an end to the generals' violation of their neighboring countries, one way or another. The rulers of the east were pleased with the king of Toufan's expressions and gradually conveyed to him that they must cumulatively send a final ultimatum to the king of Fars demanding respect for their laws and, more importantly, to stop the generals' activities. Otherwise, they would be forced to take action themselves. The rulers to the east of Fars were overly confident and wanted to go to war as soon as possible in order to finish the king of kings and take over his empire before it was too late. The king of Toufan was more cautious and, despite pressure from his people, high priests, court ministers, and generals, decided to wait and observe the accomplishments of the east region against Fars, if in fact they proceeded with their threats.

The king of Fars was informed of these activities and therefore summoned a small yet very efficient army of his most trusted guards called Javidan (meaning "guardians of infinity") and attacked and conquered Mantik quickly. He immediately annexed and then announced the attachment of Mantik to his empire. He brought law and order to Mantik but increased taxes and decreased social freedom to be able to control Mantik with a small army until security was established. He declared that the other rulers to the south and southeast of Mantik would enjoy his gracious pardon if they put down their weapons, pledged their allegiance to fighting shoulder to shoulder with the Fars army against enemies when called upon, paid their back taxes, and continued to be loyal to Fars. Most of those rulers accepted the king of king's conditions because, otherwise, they would be defeated and either killed or taken as slaves and probably offered to the generals against whom they rose. They decided that was not a choice, and it was better to serve the king as free men than the generals as slaves. Few of these rulers did not accept those conditions and became bandits and wanted by the law and lived incognito as thieves and insignificant outlaws. They preserved previous correspondence with the king of Toufan, hoping someday to be of help to them.

The king of Fars had received intelligence that to the west, some rulers and particularly the king of Toufan previously communicated with the fugitive rulers to the east to convey sympathetic gestures. The king of Toufan had conquered many smaller countries and created an empire of his own; therefore, the king of Fars needed the majority of his military for war against him in case conflict arose.

Having settled Mantik, the king of Fars called upon his generals and instructed them to quietly get the army ready, strong enough, and large enough to defeat Toufan to the west if and when necessary. He instructed his generals to increase their activities of visiting the west and especially Toufan's nearby territories to collect information, intelligence, women, and horses in order to weaken the enemy's security and abilities. He warned them not to increase their activities to the level that would make the kings to the west and particularly the king of Toufan liable to defend their countries and people and therefore forced to enter into war prematurely. He guided them to balance their activities in a manner that would weaken those rulers but not aggressively enough to evoke war out of desperation.

Generals, pleased with king's decision, accelerated their visits to the west and frequently fought small battles only to bring a large number of horses and women. They mostly killed a small number of young militants because they did not find them trustworthy any longer. The killings also reduced Toufan's ability to draft young and strong warriors. They were afraid of the Fars army and therefore reluctant to join that of Toufan.

The king of Toufan was a just king himself whose policies mostly paralleled with that of the king of Fars because Toufan, like Fars, believed in the teachings of the Good Book of the god of gods, the god of light. He was aware of such increased visits but did not dare to start a war with Fars. So he ordered his spies and trusted subordinates to visit Fars anonymously for espionage and see what they could get, be it gold, women, or information. He ordered them to stir things up in Fars but not to the level to invoke war with Toufan.

The Fars empire grew to the east, and the fortunes of Mantik added to her strength and wealth significantly. The wisdom of the king of kings and the wealth and strength of Fars convinced the king of Toufan to avoid war until a more opportune situation arose. Meanwhile, his people, court ministers, and generals increased their pressure by expressing their dissatisfaction with such policies and wanted more affirmative action. The king of Toufan realized that war with Fars was gradually becoming inevitable yet still thought Toufan was not ready and waited for the proper time and situation. He did not want to reduce or lose his chances by starting a war immaturely, unprepared and without certainty about victory.

Meanwhile, after a long absence, the king of Mantik returned to his country, only to find out that the king of Fars had conquered Mantik, raised taxes, and reduced social freedom and wealth. The king of Fars had set a prize for his head, and bounty hunters were looking for him. Fearful for his life, he escaped to a temple in the mountains and became a priest himself.

CHAPTER FIVE

IMPERFECTION

Among the generals of Fars, one was closer to the king and therefore more powerful compared with the other generals. He was the king of several countries and had significant military capabilities with a substantial amount of wealth. However, he did not have any children and was weary that after he died, there was no son to replace him. He exhausted all remedies within his power, from taking the high priests' advice to setting a considerable prize for cure, but to no avail. At times he lost all hopes and became desperate, but his wife insisted he continue his efforts. She believed they would eventually find the cure. The general did not wish to adopt any child. He believed that only the child whose blood was from him would be able to rule after his passing. He often stayed up all night and thought about finding a remedy to his dilemma. He emotionally suffered immensely for the lack of a son, especially when confronted by other generals having more than one. His wife told him the king of kings was the only person who could possibly help him, and he must request his help. The general was reluctant and resisted his wife for many years, but he was getting older and more and more anxious. He realized his time was running fast; hence, there were fewer chances for him to have a succession.

He therefore requested a private meeting with the king of kings. The king gave him permission to speak in private. The general explained his dilemma and prayed to the king for his wisdom and power to help him. The king told him he would do anything within his power, which was quite considerable. He was optimistic to solve the general's problem shortly. The king also told him he should not have waited all these years and, in the future, to come to him promptly when confronting a dilemma. The general was increasingly grateful and apologized for keeping a secret from his favored king.

The king secretively sent messengers all around the kingdom to find a cure for the general's hindrance. The king promised a huge amount of gold, wealth, and power to whoever either could cure the general's impediment or knew somebody who could find the cure. The purpose was to find a cure to enable his general to have children and particularly a son.

So the messengers went to the east and west far and wide to find the answer. One of them came to Mantik and received information that the previous king was the only person who ever went to the northern mountain to kill Seepar and came back alive. But his whereabouts was unknown. After further investigation, he discovered that the king of Mantik had become a priest living in a temple in the mountains to the north. There was also an indication of Seepar's demise since the Mantik's fortunes and wealth had gone to Fars. He presumed the king must have either killed Seepar or brought back with him something of significance belonging to Seepar. Hence, the messenger informed the king of kings of his findings. The king immediately called on the general and notified him of the good news. The king of kings wanted to bring the king of Mantik, now a priest, to his court for interrogation. He wanted to attain any and all information the priest might have obtained during his journey to the mountains. More notably, if he was able to cure the general, his life would be spared, and he would be given anything he wanted. The general requested permission to speak, which was granted. He courteously said the priest had been a king himself, and if the king of kings gave his word to generously grant him his wish, he would ask for his country back, which was a significant source of wealth for Fars at the time a war with Toufan was imminent. He believed they could not force him to cure the general if he did not want to and in fact might cause damage. Therefore, he prayed to the king to allow the general and his wife to go to the priest to explain their dilemma and seek help. The king agreed, and the general and his wife traveled anonymously to Mantik and then to the temple where the priest was said to be living. They asked permission to see the priest and were received by him. The priest asked for the reason or reasons they traveled to the temple. They explained their cause and asked for his wisdom to cure them. The priest told them to go back to where they came from as the only way for them to have a son would not result in what they wanted. The general told the priest he would spend the rest of his life and wealth to raise a just and fair son, one that would serve more than rule. The priest told them the sequence of events would be beyond their control and that this son, if born alive at all, would cause much agony for them and more problems rather than healing any pain. But the general and his wife did not want to accept anything less than a son and therefore closed eyes to the priest's proclamation. They simply assumed the priest did not know about their wealth and power and therefore took them as ordinary people.

The priest, on the other hand, having lost three sons to Seepar and his kingdom to the king of Fars, was eager to find some way to take revenge against them and possibly kill Seepar or have it killed, wash himself in its blood, and then achieve his long lost goal of defeating Fars and ruling the world. So upon the insistence of the general and his wife, he told them he may be able to help but only once. In return they must convince the king of Fars to return his country to him. The general told him that was impossible because the king would not give back Mantik even for the sake of his best and closest general. The general continued that the countries beyond Mantik were then a part of the Fars kingdom. Fars needed Mantik to access and rule them. Furthermore, the priest was not in a position to make demands from the king of Fars since his head was wanted, and more noticeably, the king of kings knew about his whereabouts but assured him of the king's generosity if he cooperated.

The priest accepted the general's offer subject to receiving a pardon order from the king himself. The general sent messengers to the king, and the king accepted the conditions and sent a royal order, sufficient gold, and other valuables to the priest. The priest was very pleased because according to the conditions of the pardon, he was a free man, the temple maintained its sovereignty, and nobody could enter the temple grounds without his permission as long as he confined himself to it, a small kingdom by itself. He could start raising a small army to begin with and then secretly go to the mountains for the second time in order to kill Seepar. This time he was more experienced and therefore had a much better chance to succeed.

Upon the arrival of the king's pardon, the priest took the small fraction of Seepar's fingernail he had saved for years and made a powder of it. He then dissolved the powder in a glass of wine. He gave the glass of wine to the general and charged that he and his wife must drink the wine together at the same time to become one. So they did and then went back to Fars.

To their surprise, the general's wife became pregnant, and the court's high priests predicted it would be a boy. The king of kings ordered new gold coins to be minted commemorating the festivities. The king ordered ceremonies throughout the country and invited the king of Toufan to the royal ceremony as a gesture of friendship. He planned to speak with the king of Toufan to express his disapproval of the generals' takings and his desire to enter into a peace treaty under the conditions of which the eastern part of Toufan neighboring Fars would be attached to his kingdom. In return he would waive taxes on the attached territories and would prevent the generals' activities.

The king of Toufan knew this invitation was about more than celebrating the general's joyful news; hence, he sent back his gratuities but respectfully declined the invitation, expressing there existed some urgent matters in his country he must attend to personally.

After nine months, nine days, and nine hours, the general's wife gave birth to a healthy and strong boy in the middle of the night. The boy was bigger than any newborn they had ever seen. Other than the size, he looked normal except his left hand had only four fingers, looking like an eagle's Talon. The fingers had long and sharp claws that could easily tear the side of his cradle.

The general recalled notion of Mantik's priest and inquired the advice of the high priests. They said the king of Mantik must have sold his soul to the gods of darkness and this boy was born of the darkness; therefore, he must be destroyed at once. In the middle of the night, the general quietly took the boy to the desert and left him there to be eaten by beasts. Upon returning to his palace, he ordered his spies to find a dead newborn male and bring the boy to him. The spies found a dead newborn and brought his corpse to the general. The general then informed the king that the boy was born dead and he was mourning his loss. The king ordered seven weeks of mourning throughout the country for the death of the general's son.

CHAPTER SIX

SKIES HELP

In the desert in the middle of the night, the newborn was surrounded by beasts that were to feast on him shortly. It was dark, cold, and quiet in the desert, but the newborn could see the eyes of the beasts around him shining under the moonlight. In his dismay, he could not defend himself and could not escape. The child could not even cry since his voice would direct the beasts to his demise. He closed his eyes and quietly waited for the sharp teeth of the beasts to rip into his fragile and helpless body.

But suddenly and faster than thunder, a bright light appeared from above in the middle of the darkness and took him to the skies. The newborn, in his unawareness, realized his life was to be finished and that now he was in the presence of a power beyond his understanding. He imagined being taken to the big bird's nest and fed to its hungry chicks. As the giant and ferocious bird took him higher and higher, his hopes for survival dipped lower and lower. When the bird arrived at the vicinity of the top of the highest mountain, he saw the bedrock and imagined it as a sacrificial platform. It was cold and dark beyond imagination, and he was about to freeze. But what was the difference whether he froze to death or was fed to the big bird's chicks? Yet he thought freezing would be less painful, so without a word, he prayed with all his heart and soul.

"God, give me my wish and freeze me to death," he thought. "Grant me the first and only wish I made in my short life if you exist. If not, then to hell with you." Nevertheless, he did not realize he would be granted more than he bargained for.

The little boy, gradually becoming numb, thought, "What a pity." Within a few hours of his birth, he already suffered more pain and agony than most people of the Fars empire did in their entire lives. He could not understand why his parents did not want him, and worse, they practically fed him to the animals of the darkness. He had not done anything but to come to life. In his unawareness, he could not find any rationality for such heartless and cruel behavior. If his parents did not want him, why did they conceive him? Maybe this was the way humans served the big and strong bird, probably their god or some type of correspondent to their god. Whatever the reason, he was chosen to be sacrificed, and there was nothing he could do about it. Instinctively, he desired to live because life could be sweet even through the agony he was put in, but not for him—not during short few hours since he was born. He was never to be protected or sheltered just like all other children. He would never know the meaning of success or defeat nor the warmth of love in his heart. The only sensation he had experienced was resentment and hatred from his parents within few seconds of his birth, or maybe even before he was born. But now it was too late for him. He simply closed his eyes and waited for whatever was going to happen to him. He expected nothing short of an awful and slow death.

Seepar, on the other hand, had felt part of it in the boy and took upon itself to save, protect, and raise what was made of him. Seepar took the boy to its place on top of the highest mountain, fed him, and kept him warm under its feathers. Seepar called the boy Zesht (meaning "ugly") and raised him as its own until the age of seven. Seepar taught the boy all the wisdom it had and showed him all the powers it had. Zesht spent most of his time understanding the meaning and source of power and strength; that life was imperfect. Seepar told him life and death were two sides of the same phenomenon. Without one, the other would not exist. He learned that the intrinsic attribute of life was to be born, to live, and someday to die, and no being could scape death. Even Seepar would pass someday. He learned that Seepar's nature required it to feed on the young and strong if it wanted to live. However, its life spread the fortunes of right and wrong. Seepar taught him that without wrong, right would not exist and vice versa; however, his choices would make the difference between the two. Zesht learned to be self-sufficient, to provide for and to protect himself, and to always do within his power what he believed was right. He learned to be brave yet cautious, to be kind but not to foolishly trust others, and above all to trust his own feelings and beliefs—to come to understand that his feelings would never lie to him but could be misunderstood by him. Seepar told him to refer to his roots whenever in doubt and to do what these principles taught him.

So many days and so many nights passed, and Zesht became stronger and wiser—a child who learned about life and death from the moment he was born.

CHAPTER SEVEN

Return to Civilization

Upon the last day of his seventh year, Seepar told Zesht it was time for him to go back to humans as he belonged to them by nature. Zesht was happy living with Seepar and did not wish to leave. He told Seepar these humans were the ones who left an innocent newborn in the desert to die. What would they do to him now? Seepar answered there was no other way for him but to go back to humans where his essence was, regardless of how they treated him, because with Seepar, he was neither human nor Seepar. He must remember Seepar would always be with him through its spirit. Seepar then gave him three of its feathers and told him whenever he needed help, to go atop of an elevated land and then burn one of the feathers, and Seepar's spirit would appear to help him. Seepar told Zesht that as a human, he was the son of a powerful king of Fars, second only to the king of kings; nevertheless, he had parts of Seepar both genetically and spiritually, and that was the reason his father left him in the desert. It described that when Zesht was born, other humans saw the signs of greatness in him, and that frightened them. They were confronted with a new breed that they could not understand or relate to; therefore, they did not tolerate his existence, which otherwise could have forced them to live in fear for as long as he lived. The roots of their fear were their own weakness inside, which caused their hatred and drove them to eliminate him once and for all. Seepar suggested to Zesht to cover his left hand to avoid problems in the future since humans were not bothered with what they could not see or hear. It also advised Zesht to learn from his experience, to use humans' weaknesses and hatred to his advantage, but warned him that fear and hatred were strong drives, the kind of dark forces that could push men to derive achievements of unprecedented proportions.

Zesht sat on Seepar's back and asked it to take him for a flight one last time. Seepar accepted, and as it flew, Zesht wept with all his heart. He said farewell to all the beings in that place where he had lived his entire life.

Zesht reluctantly left Seepar and headed back to Fars but went to a remote section of the country where he was far away from the rule of his biological father. He followed Seepar's guidance and worked hard, and as he grew older, he learned better to conceal his left hand—the source of fear for people. Zesht gradually saved some wealth and established himself in the community as an honest and fair man whose achievements were made available through hard work, adherence to the principles of the god of light, and generosity. He was generous to other people with his wealth and with his soul. He gave to others without expectations and helped those in need. He regularly went to the temple of the god of light to pray and to serve as best as he could.

Zesht, in his frequent visits, noticed one of the mistresses in the temple of the god of light who was always praying and serving with a smile. She made his heart pound. He was eager to talk to her but did not wish to break her silence, and it mostly sufficed to just watch her. One afternoon after his prayers, he decided to walk about the temple grounds in solitude and think. As he was walking away from the temple, he heard a woman calling him from behind. He turned around and saw the girl from the temple following him. She walked up to him and introduced herself as Forough (meaning "ray of light"). She asked him about his name. Zesht told her his name. She said she had seen him often in the temple, but he never said a word. Zesht could not speak and was just staring at her. After a long pause, he said he did not wish to break her silence and that he found peace in her presence. They talked and laughed together for some time and became friends.

Zesht soon fell in love with her and thereafter married her. Forough was devoted to serving the god of light and goodness. She did not care about Zesht's left hand or what other people thought of him. In fact she believed Zesht's left hand was a source of power and therefore marked by the character of the god of gods, the god of light. After a while, Forough became pregnant, and the priests predicted it was a boy.

Meanwhile, Forough's health was deteriorating as she got closer to delivering her child. According to the priests and doctors, the child was too big and consumed all the nutrition and energy her body could produce. They warned Zesht of the great danger the child could impose on Forough's health; she might not survive the child's birth.

Zesht frequently talked to Forough and suggested to rid her of such danger, but she did not agree. On the night before she was going to deliver her child, she lost all her strength. She realized death was asking for her. Zesht was sitting next to her, holding her hand. Zesht was quietly crying. He told her he did not want the child if it was at the expense of her life. She was the only person who ever cared for him and the only person he deeply ever cared for. Forough told him her child had the marks of gods, and he must promise to her to take care of him or her the best he could. Zesht did not want the child, but Forough insisted that he grant her last wish so she could die peacefully and, therefore, her soul be accepted by the god of light. Zesht, forced by Forough's insistence, made the promise shortly before her passing. Zesht hoped deep inside for the child yet to be born to die with Forough. He did not want to see the face of the child as any resemblance between them would be a knife to his heart every time he looked at the child. He did not want to face this child in a hateful state of mind and emotions. He prayed all night for the child to be born dead. All of this reminded him of his own birth. Now he could understand his own parents better but knew he was not to kill or have his child killed. That was the reason he wished for the child to be born dead.

HAGHDAR

Despite Zesht's prayers, the boy survived and came to life early morning next day before the dawn. Zesht, mourning Forough's passing all night, told his servants he was not ready to see the newborn. Yet the servants told him he must see the boy as he was not an ordinary child. They were fearful the child might bring bad luck to all. They told Zesht it was not an infant but rather a monster, the size of a three-year-old boy.

Zesht, weary of his own childhood, went to see the newborn. He examined the child carefully and realized there was nothing abnormal about him except his size and masculinity at birth. During Zesht's examination, the boy extended his hand and grabbed one of Zesht's fingers on his right hand and squeezed it so hard, only to break it. He then grabbed another finger of Zesht but did not break it, showing he punished Zesht once for one sin he committed—wishing him dead.

The size, the strength, and the wisdom of the newborn was beyond what Zesht had anticipated. He wanted to erase the boy but kept hearing Forough's voice and the promise he made to her. Promise. Promise. Promise. So Zesht left the newborn to his servants to raise and took a journey to the farthest part of Fars.

The servants called the newborn Haghdar (meaning "I am right") and raised him as their own. Haghdar grew bigger and bigger and stronger and stronger. At age nine, there escaped a lion from captivity and ran into the town, killing several persons. Nobody dared to stop the mad lion. Haghdar was sleeping when awakened by the noise from the crowd. The servants told him to take cover in a safe place just like everybody else. He refused to do so and came out looking for the lion. The lion was running around when suddenly it saw Haghdar. The lion jumped toward Haghdar in order to break his neck with one strike of its powerful paws. Haghdar dodged the strike, went behind it, and grabbed the lion's neck. He then broke its neck with lightning speed and dropped its body on his feet.

The story of his bravery spread throughout the country, and Zesht heard about it. Zesht remembered Forough's assertion and thought the boy must have the marks of gods. She must have known it since she served the god of light all her life. Thus, he decided to go back to see his son. Zesht came back to Haghdar and hugged him tightly. He said he was sorry for abandoning him and promised to never leave him again. Haghdar said he was happy to have his father by his side. He added that travel makes a man wise, and it is the attribute of wisdom that earns the respect of the others. Zesht promised to spend the rest of his life with Haghdar, not knowing what the future had bestowed upon them.

The bravery of Haghdar was brought to the attention of the king of kings, who always welcomed strong and brave young men. The king of kings summoned Haghdar. He came to the court and was received by the king. The king could not believe he was not even ten years old. He was a big and strong man seemingly in his early twenties.

Haghdar joined the king of Fars's armed forces at age ten. He became a general at age twelve and the general of generals, the most trusted general and head of Javidan at age sixteen. His fame spread throughout the world. He won every war. No man had the courage or strength to challenge him. Many warriors, once seeing him in the battlefield, escaped before the war started. Others bowed to his power. Haghdar was just, wise, and the greatest warrior the world had ever seen, the likes of whom were not seen to that day.

CHAPTER EIGHT

HERO

The king of Fars, having Haghdar by his side, was eager to enclose the rest of the world to his kingdom, to disseminate his wisdom, and to show the world his good ways of life. He intended to establish the perfect empire and perfect world ruled by the guidance of the god of light for as long as humans lived and to the end of time. He openly spoke with Haghdar about his vision, and they started to gradually make plans to achieve the king's vision of excellence and perfection, or as close to perfection as humanly possible.

One night, the king had a nightmare pertaining to the gods of darkness gaining strength through certain forces devoted to Ahreman (meaning "Mephistopheles"). These forces, in turn, would prevent him from attaining his ideals. As all nightmares, it was vague and not clear, yet it insinuated a monster coming from the sea in the middle of the darkness and ate all children in Fars. He woke up shivering and wondered what his nightmare could mean. He decided not to seek the interpretation of his nightmare from high priests. He was wary they may speak of it with others and then spread rumors and therefore diminish confidence in him and his vision. He was determined to either materialize his vision or meet his demise on his way to it.

The king then went to the largest and most believed temple of the god of light in Fars and knelt before the old book. After rendering the rituals, he inquired from the god of light about the wisdom of his nightmare. The king was true to himself and true to the god of light. He cried all night. Early in the morning just before the dawn, in the middle of sleep and awareness, the king thought he heard a voice saying, "The Sea of Fars." He then woke up and thanked the god of light for giving him prudence and went back to his palace.

The Fars borders to the South ended by waters called the Sea of Fars. To the south and beyond the Sea of Fars, there were certain warriors who were brutal and savage. They did not organize a country but instead a group of murderous warriors who attacked different places, especially wealthy cities within the Fars kingdom neighboring the Sea of Fars, killed everybody on their way and stole their food, gold, and anything else they could get their hands on. They also captured young men and women as slaves. They never worked and spent all their lives either at war or training for war. They attacked in the middle of the night, killed many, took their possessions, and left all before the break of the day. People living in those territories of Fars had often complained to the king, arguing their territories were the only section of the Fars empire not being protected by the kingdom. They paid their taxes and therefore were entitled to the protection of the king.

The king had many issues at hand in more important lands in the east and the west; hence, he never considered to fight the savages until the morning of the nightmare. Upon having the nightmare and guidance of the god of light, the king decided it was time to settle the old account with these servants of the gods of darkness.

The king called on Haghdar and his generals to discuss and plan the war against those agents of the gods of darkness. Haghdar was fourteen years old at that time yet one of the higher-ranked generals. Generals assured the king they were able to defeat and destroy savage warriors, yet the king told them he would personally lead the campaign.

The king raised a considerably sized army consisting of his best soldiers, including members of Javidan, and campaigned to the south. It was a long journey yet worthy of his time and effort. He appointed his oldest son, Haghdar's friend, to govern with the help of a council comprised of high priests and court ministers until his return.

The warriors to the south of the Sea of Fars received information that the king of Fars himself was leading the army to the war against them. The leader of the savages was a ruthless warrior in his late thirties. He had been to many battles and single-handedly destroyed many of the opposing military troops. He was big and strong with no concern for others. He killed many of his warriors out of anger or mistrust. No man had ever defeated him in a one-on-one combat. He was cruel and fierce and knew only one thing—destruction.

He rounded up his warriors and told them their day of victory was arriving, that the king of Fars was personally leading the army to his death. Once they killed the king of Fars and destroyed his army, they would rule the world, and nothing could stop them thereafter. He said this war was their chance of a thousand years and may not be spared as it might not ever happen again. He went to the temple of the gods of darkness and sought wisdom. The high priests told him the gods of darkness favored him.

Hence, the two sides met, and the war continued for seven months. The savages were fully familiar with the battleground since it was their home. They also were highly motivated to defeat Fars and therefore rule the world. The war was the bloodiest the king of Fars had ever conducted, and there was no sign of progress on either side. At the end of the seventh month, both sides having lost many warriors, the leader of the savages sent a message to the king of Fars. In the message, he reflected this war was mainly between him and the king. They both knew they wanted to rule the world their way. Therefore, it would be senseless to shed more blood. In view of this fact, he offered one warrior from each side, one representing Fars and the other the savages, to fight to death. The winner of the fight would represent the winner of the war, and the other side would submit to the winner.

The king of Fars knew about the leader of the savages. Without doubt he would be the warrior on their side. He called on Haghdar in private and discussed the message from the leader of the savages with him. The king told him the savages were agents of the gods of darkness and must be destroyed. The king was always just and generous to the people of the lands he conquered; however, this was one war that could not be won with graciousness. This was one war they could not afford to lose no matter the collateral damages, even if the king himself had to fight the leader of the savages. He then asked Haghdar for the name, among the rank and file, of the person he thought was most suitable for the critical task at hand. Haghdar asked permission to speak freely, which was granted. Haghdar said he was disappointed at the king to underestimate the loyalty and power of such loyalty among his subjects. Haghdar then prayed to the king to allow him to fight the leader of the savages, to reply with the message that his offer was accepted. Haghdar promised the king with his life to win the fight for Fars yet warned that the army must stand guard as the savages never kept a promise and could not be trusted.

Early next day, the two warriors, the leader of the savages and Haghdar, met for the first time in the battlefield. The fight took seven days. At the end of the seventh day, a severely injured Haghdar defeated the leader of the savages, laid him on the ground, and sat on his chest to finish him. Haghdar pulled out his knife to kill the leader of the savages slowly and with disgrace—a painful and prolonged death to reflect on the savage warriors, so painful he would beg for his death.

The leader of the savages said, with a very weak and trembling voice, "Take off your hood and let me see your face." Haghdar removed his iron hood and then removed the warrior's hood. They looked at each other eye to eye for a few very long seconds. The leader of the savages asked Haghdar for his name. Haghdar told him his name. He said he never heard of him. What was the name of his father? he asked. Haghdar said Zesht. He declared, the greatest warrior ever lived was killed at the hands of Haghdar, son of Zesht. Haghdar thought for a few seconds and then pronounced, "For that I will not kill you in disgrace and will not take your honor away. You will die with honor and be buried according to your traditions with full courtesy." He then pushed his knife into his heart for a quick death.

The savages could not believe the turn of events. They had not heard of Haghdar and did not know who Fars's warrior was. After a long pause, one of them screamed they were all warriors and leaders and might not lose the chance of ruling the world and so ordered others to attack. They fought for seven more days until the savages were completely destroyed and the Fars kingdom extended to the lands beyond the Sea of Fars. The king ordered a full funeral for the savages' leader according to their tradition and attended the funeral with Haghdar by his side.

Upon returning to his court, the king appointed Haghdar as the head of the generals and Javidan—the highest rank, only junior to the king and the prince. The king also ordered seven weeks of celebration in honor of Haghdar and his victory, the glory of Fars kingdom.

CHAPTER NINE

Rise of Toufan

While the Fars army fought savages, the king of Toufan added countries to his empire and raised a strong and efficient army. Tired of the Fars generals' visits to his country and the taking of young and horses and under pressure by his people, court ministers, and especially priests—who still thought Haghdar was a descendant of the gods of darkness and afraid he might overtake Toufan—he sent a message to the king of Fars, requesting to be recognized only second to the Fars empire. Toufan had conquered many countries to the west and established order over all countries ruled. The king of Toufan was brave and wise, and his policies governing Toufan and conquered lands were in line with those of the king of Fars in respect to fairness and justice. He sent gold and valuable gifts with the message that Toufan desired to be at peace with Fars. Fars and Toufan would divide the world between them—Fars to rule the east, the richer and wider part of the world, and Toufan to the west. The two countries would accept each other's boundaries and live as neighbors with mutual respect. Particularly, the king of kings would restrain his generals from visiting Toufan.

The king called upon Haghdar and sought his opinion. Haghdar, offended by the demand from the king of Toufan, stated, "Your Majesty, the king of kings, today he makes demand. Tomorrow he will issue orders. There must be a line beyond which the king of Toufan may not pass. This is clearly that line."

The king nodded, concurring with Haghdar. Haghdar continued, "Old accounts must be settled, but only by an appropriate apology from the king of Toufan and a promise to abide by the laws and rules of Fars as far as a subordinate king is concerned." The king of kings was pleased with Haghdar's point of view. He had quietly prepared the army for some time to confront Toufan. So he called upon the messengers and told them the king of Toufan must be grateful to the king of kings allowing him to build his empire, yet he was not in the position to make demands. The king of Fars declared that he expected the king of Toufan to express his loyalty to him once again and the commitment to send an army to accommodate Fars whenever he was called upon. He also proclaimed that the loyalty of the king of Toufan was the only message he expected to receive; hence, he disbursed all his gifts to the servants of his generals—an insult a king in the throne might not endure. Further, to add salt to injury and as a symbol of offense, the king of Fars sent a small army to attach to his country the part of Toufan next neighboring Fars. The region with the most beautiful women and best horses in the world, so it was said.

Fars's small army took over that part of Toufan without any incident as the king of Toufan still did not feel it was time to go to war with Fars. The Fars army arrested Toufan's generals ruling that part of their country as well, and sent the captured Toufan's generals to the court of the king of kings alive. The king of kings received Toufan's captured generals in his court personally and treated them fairly and with respect. He then had them under house arrest in mansions near his palace and ordered the guards to treat them with respect and to provide them what they wished. However, they were not to escape or leave their quarters at all costs except by the king's order.

CHAPTER TEN

ENEMY COUNSELING

The king of Fars occasionally sent messages to Toufan's captured generals, indicating his wish to counsel with them at their discretion. Toufan's generals did not know what plan the king of Fars had in mind and were fearful of him. Therefore, they avoided him to the extent possible. The king of kings never forced them to accommodate him. On appropriate occasions, he invited Toufan's captured generals to some of the royal ceremonies. During these ceremonies, they were allowed to go anywhere permitted by the palace rules. Further, they were allowed to speak or refuse to speak if they chose to do so.

Gradually, the generals acknowledged the generosity and justice of the king of kings and discussed it between themselves. Some of them had married and settled in Fars. Those who had their children born in Fars could leave their quarters for short periods of time and to short distances accompanied by their specially appointed servants.

The king of Fars advised Toufan's generals that in his country, everybody must be useful and perform useful work. Even the elderly must have a useful task, and it was the kingdom's responsibility to create a proper work environment for whoever lived in Fars, whether free or in captivity. And therefore, the job of the generals was to draw plans for hypothetical wars and see through them. The generals were expected to do their best to win these hypothetical wars by utilizing an army that was defined by the king himself. The battlefield for these wars and the number of soldiers and army amenities were given to them by the king of Fars. The generals had to make their plans within the limitations the king allotted them as far as the place of battles, army size, and capabilities were concerned.

The generals mostly had not been out of their quarters for years. They were told Fars and Toufan had signed a peace treaty, and all previous conflicts were forgotten and forgiven on either side.

The king of Fars, to ascertain the geographic location of the hypothetical battles and the amount of artillery allotted to each general in order to plan the imaginary wars, would make certain cosmetic changes to Toufan's maps of territories and the amount of their artilleries and then give them to the generals for their projects. They never realized they were helping the king of Fars to wager war against their own country.

So the generals completed these war projects and did their best supposing the two countries had resolved their differences and lived in peace. One of the generals once asked the king of Fars that if the two countries were at peace with one another, why would he not let them go back to their own country? The king of Fars responded that he had grown fond of them and did not wish them harm. According to Toufan laws, they would be executed for being captured by the Fars army alive and still living with affluence when their soldiers were killed, their people lived in relative poverty and were ruled by an invading army.

CHAPTER ELEVEN

INTERIM DEFEAT

The king of Fars was so absorbed in his vision of conquering and attaching the entire world to his empire that he somewhat lost insight for his army located in Toufan's occupied territories and their ability, or lack of it thereof, to defeat that country if and when it should become necessary. He concluded he was getting older, and this opportunity most likely was his last chance to unite the world, particularly Toufan, under Fars's flag.

On the other hand, the king of Toufan had received information that the king of Fars was raising an army to seek war, and in fact, if he did not go to war, Fars would bring the war to Toufan. Thus, in order to push back the Fars army already invading parts of Toufan, he raised a relatively small yet extremely efficient army slightly larger than the Fars army invading Toufan's territories and appointed one of his junior generals to lead the campaign and defeat and force Fars's army out of that section of his country. The king of Toufan knew the king of Fars would not send reinforcement troops and supplies to help these generals with limited abilities in those territories. He was raising an army for the ultimate war with Toufan. The king of Fars did not want to take any premature risk of losing more of his soldiers at this time other than those who already were stationed in Toufan's territories. Further, the king of kings expected his army already in Toufan to be able to defeat and destroy Toufan's small army before the start of the final war. The king of Fars was on the assumption that such defeat would be devastating to Toufan's army and its confidence as they had not lost a war in so many years.

The king of Toufan, before campaigning against the Fars army, sent separate messages to the Fars generals and invited them to join him. He reasoned that the king of Fars did not care about them any longer. He left them to be killed or taken as slaves by his army. He argued that it was the king of Fars who turned his back on them, and therefore there would be no shame for them to join Toufan. He promised they would be treated as generals once they proved their loyalty to the king of Toufan by helping him to defeat Fars army and push them out of his country.

Most Fars generals rejected his offer and sent messages back to the king of Toufan, declaring their allegiance belonged to the Fars. Nevertheless, some of the generals had lived in Toufan for years and were married to Toufanian women. They had children who were born in and citizens of Toufan. These children were raised under the values of Toufan. Most particularly, three of the generals, dissatisfied with the lack of support from the king of Fars and under pressure by their wives and children, accepted the offer and defected to Toufan. The king of Toufan warmly welcomed them and appointed them to his top team of generals, who basically drew the war strategy and tactics. The generals had valuable information about Fars's army capabilities and tactics and submitted them to the king of Toufan. Upon acquiring precious information and the drawing of the war plans, he ordered the movement of the troops led by his junior general. He then secretly disguised himself as one of his army's cavaliers and joined the troops yet announced he was going to vacation as he was certain his junior general was more than capable to defeat and destroy Fars's army residing in Toufan.

The Fars generals ruling that part of Toufan were overly confident with the fact that their small army had already defeated Toufan in the past evidenced by occupying their land; did not think much of war planning and appeared at the battlegrounds casually. They had received messages from the king of Fars that upon the destruction of Toufan's army, they would be generously rewarded.

The Fars generals believed Toufan's small army, led by a junior general, was not a real show of force. They reckoned Toufan did not intend to actually go to war with Fars and probably would desire to negotiate. They also believed if the war escalated, the king of Fars would have Haghdar campaigning against Toufan, and they did not believe the king of Toufan would dare to take such risk. Their evaluation of the campaign at hand was that Toufan's junior general would either wish to negotiate or, in the remote possibility of war, be defeated. They planned to subsequently attach another part of Toufan to Fars. They assumed the king of Fars would be greatly pleased with their performance and, as promised, would reward them with substantial wealth and power and might even appoint one of them as the king of Toufan.

So the Toufan and Fars armies confronted each other. The war took seven days, and the Fars army was defeated and destroyed; its generals were either killed or captured by Toufan's army. The king of Toufan, after defeating the Fars army and taking back occupied parts of his country, secretly and quickly went back to his court and announced he was back from vacation and prepared to receive his victorious army coming back from war. The king of Toufan received his army in a majestic ceremony, and his generals presented Fars's captured generals in chains. To humiliate the king of Fars, the king of Toufan had Fars's generals beheaded and their heads sent to the king of kings in a cheap and ragged piece of cloth with the message "Stay where you are and stay alive. There is nothing awaiting the Fars army in Toufan except captivity, humiliation, and death."

CHAPTER TWELVE

The Reception

The king of Fars received the report of the defeat of his army and that certain Toufan messengers were bringing the heads of his generals to him as a gesture of humiliation. He knew some of the heads belonged to Haghdar's good friends. He would be very angry and might interfere with his plans. Haghdar had volunteered to help the generals before the fight with Toufan started, but the king denied his plea. So he called on Haghdar and told him some of the countries to the east had found out about Fars's defeat by Toufan. They assumed Haghdar was needed in the west and therefore would not be able to attend the east affairs. Accordingly, they were rioting, and some even spread rumors that Haghdar was killed in that war. The king advised him to go to the east with a small yet effective troop to show them the punishment for treason and the spreading of rumors was severe. Haghdar knew about Toufan's messengers bringing the head of his friends but did not say anything and accepted the mission. He left with a small troop of one thousand men.

A few days later, the messengers of the king of Toufan arrived at the palace of the king of Fars with the heads of the generals in a piece of ragged cloth. They appeared before the king of kings and paid their respects to the great king. The king of Fars ordered Toufan's captured generals to attend the reception of the messengers. They were positioned in the balcony, where they could not talk to or contact the messengers but could see them and hear their conversation with the king.

The chief messenger, after rendering customary pleasantries, requested permission to speak, which was granted. He exclaimed, "Your Majesty, we accepted this mission with the knowledge that we will not much longer live. We have accepted this fact and are ready to face our gods. However, we request permission to relay our king's message to you before meeting death. We also pray to Your Majesty to meet death at the hands of Haghdar. There is no greater honor than to be killed by the hands of the great warrior, which in turn will place us in history's pages. Further, our death by the hands of Haghdar will disprove rumors that he is no longer alive."

The king of Fars asked for the message, and the messengers opened the ragged cloth and dropped the generals' heads on the palace floor at the feet of the king. They then said it was best for Fars's army to stay away, and if they campaigned against Toufan, they should expect nothing more than humiliation, defeat, and death.

The king thought deeply for few seconds. He then declared, "The king of kings does not, and neither do his subjects, kill messengers. They do not kill captivated generals either. They, in fact, treat them with respect. Haghdar is away on special mission. However, even if he were here, he would not disgrace this palace by the blood of the likes of the messengers of the disgraced king. Haghdar killed enemies and devotees of the Ahreman only in the battlefield. The messengers will have to find other ways to go into the pages of history as their king will. Alternatively, they may choose to face Haghdar in the battlefield, only to be killed and sent to the deepest parts of the darkness, a symbol of the lowest of the low. Now, go back to Toufan, and tell your master he will be severely punished for his sinister and devious action."

CHAPTER THIRTEEN

MAGICIAN

Haghdar went to the east and quickly established order, made sure Fars's appointed kings ruling those regions were in a strong and stable position, and came back to the court. The king of kings informed him of the progress of the events and that they must now enter into military conflict with Toufan. He asked Haghdar to raise an army the likes of which had never existed, to campaign against and defeat Toufan and bring the head of their king in a piece of ragged cloth not any better than the one in which the messengers brought the heads of his generals. The king also told him to be firm with soldiers and fair to the people of Toufan. His plan was to finish Toufan's warriors who were fighting against the Fars empire, draft soldiers who were willing to fight for Fars, and be just to the people; to provide freedom, happiness, and wealth for them and ultimately to enclose Toufan to the Fars empire forever, both physically and spiritually.

Haghdar raised the army and became ready for the campaign. The king advised him to meet with Toufan's captured generals before departure in order to obtain further information about Toufan's king and his army, to understand the area, and to seek a suitable battleground and accessible roadways to such battlegrounds.

Haghdar set up a meeting with the generals. He told them the king of Toufan had breached the peace treaty and disgraced the king of Fars, with which they concurred. They had seen the occurrence with their own eyes from the palace terrace. Haghdar continued, however, despite their disgraceful act, the king of Fars did not wish to start a war with Toufan in order to save lives. But to restore the king's grace, he must take one thing that is most valuable to Toufan and leave it at that. If the king of Toufan accepted the taking, no blood would be shed; otherwise, he might go to war against Haghdar and the Fars army.

The generals told him there was a specific herd of wild horses living in certain territories of Toufan. The herd of horses was protected by the order of Toufan's king and was free in their territories. They were led by a horse whose strength and size was unmatchable by any standard. Toufanians frequently domesticated some of these horses, especially the older ones for reproduction. Alas, no one could get close to the leader of the horses and live as the horse was fierce and strong beyond any man's power and strength. Haghdar inquired about the localities where the wild horses lived. The generals told him their approximate location, which did not require much deviation from Haghdar's path to Toufan.

Haghdar then met with his father, Zesht, and told him he was going to accomplish the king's wish and conquer Toufan once and for all. His father advised him against being overly confident. That was the reason for the Fars army's defeat by Toufan. They exchanged farewells, and Haghdar started the campaign.

Coincidentally, Haghdar's biggest deficiency was his ride. Haghdar was so big and heavy that no ordinary horse could carry him. Some of the strongest mules from Mantik were able to carry him, but they could hardly run and were no match for the speed of a horse. Many enemy warriors escaped him in the battlefield solely because they rode faster.

Haghdar led the campaign against Toufan and concurrently looked for this leader of the wild horses. After seven weeks, they came to a vast meadow backed by heavily wooded area. Haghdar's army entered the meadow cautiously, wary of possible ambush. Haghdar rode in front of the army to lead and watch for any suspicious situation or movement.

HAGHDAR

The meadow and especially the wooded area were the places in which the wild horses had mostly been seen in the past according to Toufan's generals. Haghdar, watching every movement in the area, saw what looked like shadows in the woods for a split second but could not distinguish exactly what they were. It could have been leaves shaking by the wind, yet he knew he had to be watchful. He thought this could be a make-or-break point in his campaign.

Ironically, the wild horses and their leader were camouflaging in the woods behind the meadow. They were blending with the trees so perfectly, none of the Fars generals or soldiers saw them. However, Haghdar's eagle eyes could finally detect them. Haghdar immediately identified the leader of the horses and looked directly into its eyes. Their eyes met for the shortest time, and they simultaneously felt the mutual respect of one warrior for another. Haghdar ordered one of his soldiers to get the largest and wildest camel in the camp. Then he instructed him to put some type of special pepper under the camel's tail. This type of pepper was not edible and only used against enemies in the battlefield and, if applied accurately, would cause immense pain, make them blind, and even could cause death. He ordered soldiers to channel the camel toward the direction of the herd of horses and especially their leader after the pepper was placed under its tail. Then he ordered the rest of his army to take a short rest. Haghdar disposed himself of all weapons and his upper clothing and started walking toward the leader of the horses. The horses were on guard, waiting for their leader's command to charge. Their leader moved its tail, only to tell them to stand on guard, ready for its orders.

Meanwhile, the pain was unbearable for the camel, forcing it to run madly, stampeding some soldiers. The army gradually directed the camel toward the leader of the horses beyond the meadow. As Haghdar reached closer to the leader of the herd of horses, the camel saw him. The camel then knew its pain was inflicted by Haghdar; therefore, it charged toward him fiercely in order to seek revenge, to kill him. As the camel approached Haghdar, he stepped aside to the left with the speed of lightning and punched the camel in the head with his right fist and killed the animal on the spot. The horses were getting restless, waiting for their leader to command, which was staring at Haghdar eye to eye. Haghdar came close where he could feel its heavy breathing. He looked into its eyes and, with a soft voice nobody had ever heard from him before, said that it was the greatest warrior he had ever seen. He continued; he would treat it with respect and his army would treat it with respect, that it was free to go anywhere and to take its warriors with it at any time; however, he wished to join forces with it to make the world a better place. He then extended his right hand and touched the leader of the horses under the chin. The horse licked Haghdar's right hand as the gesture of acceptance. Haghdar said, "Your name is Raad" (meaning "thunder").

Haghdar walked back to Fars's camp with Raad on his side and the other wild horses behind them. Haghdar rounded up the army and generals. He declared his friend's name was Raad. Raad had decided to join forces with him to conquer the world together. He would respect it as a warrior only second to himself. Raad was free to go or lead its warriors anywhere it wished. He respected Raad and expected all to respect it as well. Any insult or offense against Raad would be a direct insult or offense against him. He would give his right hand to save and protect it.

There was an atmosphere of respect and strength in the air, and the entire Fars army subdued to his declaration. They realized no force in and out of this world now could match theirs both in terms of strength and spirit. The army then bowed before Raad, and Raad bowed before Haghdar, and Haghdar bowed before the army. Raad remained on its knees, and Haghdar personally saddled it and asked for permission to start their journey. Raad remained on its knees, and Haghdar elevated on to the saddle. Raad stood on its two rear legs to show their unity, size, and power. Together they were as tall and strong as a mountain. Then the two armies became one and resumed their campaign.

CHAPTER FOURTEEN

FAREWELL

Toufan was known to the world for its beautiful women. Toufan's women had moonlight-pale skin and were tall and slim yet strong. They were famous for their loyalty to their husbands and being hard workers. Women in Toufan had more or less equal rights with men, worked shoulder to shoulder with them, and participated in social activities such as business, politics, and sports. It was said that long ago, Toufan was headed by a queen, but no female had ruled Toufan in recent memory. Men came from the four corners of the world to meet and marry Toufan's women. Then again, Toufan's women loved, above all, their country and were faithful to it and except those kidnapped or taken as slaves by foreign soldiers during war time, they never left their country.

Those men who chose Toufan's women had to live in and by the laws of Toufan. Three of the Fars generals who had previously ruled Toufan's occupied territories did marry and therefore decided to live in Toufan for the rest of their lives. They were the ones who earlier defected to Toufan.

The most beautiful woman of them all was the queen, the wife of the king, named Shahrara (meaning "glory of the city"). She was from the ancestors of kings and queens for hundreds of years. In addition to the general characteristics of Toufan's women, Shahrara was well educated, sophisticated, and cultured. She had the wisdom and strength of the gods.

It was said that she was a descendant of the gods and talked to the god of beauty and love. She was not to appear in public because her presence would cause a riot and disorder. Men would do anything to have a glimpse of her. Men would kill to see her face for a second. Many men would give their lives for her smile. She smelled of a thousand roses and jasmines, with skin softer than moonlight, hair that made gold worthless, and blue eyes that calmed the ocean. She was the most valuable of Toufan, only next to the country, their gods, and their king. People of Toufan had a strong belief in her wisdom and knowledge and considered her one of the pillars based on which Toufan existed. The king was the protector of Shahrara and sought her wisdom to attend most important affairs of the country.

The night before the day the king of Toufan campaigned against Haghdar and the Fars army, the king and queen discussed the war at hand and the unity of Haghdar and Raad. Toufanians had tried for years to domesticate Raad to no avail. Once or twice they were able to rope Raad, but it did not yield and almost fought to death; therefore, they released it to maintain the order of its herd for reproduction.

Shahrara whispered that the unity of Haghdar and Raad would favor the Fars army in the war and that the king himself and the country were in grave danger. Shahrara did not wish to live without her king and prayed to join the army and, if defeated, to become a martyr rather than being captured at the hands of Fars warriors. She knew the Fars army would not have mercy on her and would keep her alive in humiliation and slavery to destroy Toufan's belief.

The king did not agree with her. He argued that Toufan's military was strong and wise. They had been training long and hard for this moment. The king and his army had conquered and adjoined many lands to Toufan, and the people of those lands now enjoyed justice and affluence in life. The king believed his empire was as large and powerful as Fars, with the difference that Fars's women were not anywhere close to Toufan's women in terms of strength, wisdom, faith, and love of their country. The king was of the belief that this was his chance to unite the world under his command and to establish the monarchy that would rule the world for thousands of years. He believed it was his time for glory; nonetheless, Fars was bringing the war to him, and there was no escape from that.

The king claimed he would not have started this war; nevertheless, he always knew it was inevitable, and sooner or later, Toufan had to defend its motherland. The Fars generals were getting more and more aggressive and each day took more of the young and the brave, be it men or women. They took Toufan's best horses, gold, and wealth, and their appetite was being fueled with greed and ease of access to what Toufan had to offer. His people, court ministers, and army generals were all dissatisfied with this situation and had repeatedly requested the king to put a stop to Fars's aggression one way or another.

He declared he had made arrangements for the queen to travel to a safe temple far away and to serve the god of light, who would protect her against all enemies until his triumphant return to the palace. They discussed past midnight. The king emphasized she might not be captured by the hands of the Fars army because her captivity would annihilate a thousand years of the Toufanians beliefs and therefore her legacy. The king added that even if Toufan were defeated and its army disseminated and disbursed, the Toufanians' belief would live as long as her legacy lived. He was certain Toufan would regain its glory as long as the Toufanians retained their belief. The queen reluctantly accepted. She cried in the arms of her king the rest of the night. Her teardrops resembled pearls floating in the clouds. Her eyes were puffed up and her heart broken. She knew deep in her heart this was the last time they would be together, and without the king, her responsibility would be immense, more than any ordinary man could bear. The next day, the king said farewell to his queen and led his army to the grand war.

CHAPTER FIFTEEN

THE BATTLE

Toufan's army was consisted of brave and well-trained warriors. The king himself was especially very experienced in war tactics and strategies. Toufan's armed forces had defeated many nations and not only knew how to fight; they also had utmost confidence in their king's wisdom and strength. Above all, they had an unbreakable love for their country. Each and every one of them was sworn to fight to the death for their homeland.

The king of Toufan chose the battleground atop a wide range of tall hills where his army held high grounds over the arriving Fars army. He ordered several of his generals to wear the king's gown and set up tents, one atop each hill, similar to his own, each of which was lodging a king. It appeared that there were numerous kings joining forces for the final combat. The king had given strict instructions to his generals to act as if they were true kings and took necessary steps to make the Fars army believe in it as well.

Haghdar and the Fars army arrived at the battlefield and camped at the foot of the hills. Haghdar's strategy was to fast attack the opposing army's heart with a small number of his best warriors while the rest of the army engaged in the war as decoy. He then would reach to their king's camp, destroy it, and kill the enemies' king. Once their king was dead, the chain of command would be disrupted, and the soldiers would not have a proper leadership. As soon as the opposing warriors realized their king was dead, they either fled the battleground or dropped their weapons and surrendered. Haghdar had won many wars with that tactic, and the Fars soldiers were well trained to do their job. In this case, he needed more warriors to attack the camp of Toufan's king since they had to fight their way uphill. Toufan's military was well positioned.

Toufan's armed forces saw Haghdar riding Raad and, for a second, shivered. They had heard about Haghdar and knew about Raad, but seeing them together as one was frightening to them.

The king of Toufan ordered one of his generals, disguised like the king, to deliver the final speech to the soldiers. The general shouted; Toufan's brave armed forces had defeated many nations who claimed to have the greatest warriors of all time. They all fell because it was not one man who won wars. It was the strength of the military and the leadership of the king that predominated others. Toufan did not have one great warrior. Toufan had one great army consisting of many like Haghdar. Further, it was not a horse to decide the fate of the war. It was the love of country, bravery, and wisdom of the king that guaranteed victory no matter who the enemy was. Amid his speech, the king cheered the general as loud as he could and said that victory would be with Toufan because their hearts were filled with love for their country. They were not there to defeat an enemy; they were there to defend their homeland, their women and children, and their ideals. He continued that every one of Toufan's warriors was willing to sacrifice their lives a hundred times rather than allowing foreigners to rule over them. The king's voice was full of hope and confidence. Toufan's army perceived the king's resolve and became very excited. They shouted, "Victory is ours, victory is ours."

Haghdar, riding Raad in front of the army, delivered his final speech before the attack. He declared that Fars was not a conqueror but rather liberator. Fars had liberated many nations and spread its good fortunes to the end of the world. Befittingly, it was time for Toufan to encounter the strength and wisdom of the messengers of freedom. He reflected to the army "To have no sympathy for those who came here to kill us, yet to be merciful to those who regret their mistake and either put down their weapons or, better yet, join the

Fars army." Fars would be victorious and would establish its high ideals in Toufan, just like all other countries liberated in the past by Fars. He noted that Fars would not rest until this mission was accomplished. This war would be written in history as one that brought freedom and happiness to the people of Toufan and unified the world. Alas, many lives would perish. He announced this was the path they should follow to make the world a better place for eternity. They would, by winning over the enemy, make their names live forever as soldiers of the god of light.

Haghdar, riding Raad, quickly attacked the heart of Toufan's army, cut through their defense lines, and arrived atop one of the hills, cut his way to the king's camp, killed the king, and quickly went back downhill, thinking the king was dead and his army would be in despair. But to his surprise, Toufan's army continued to fight and not only did not flee but also followed through down the hill and killed many of Haghdar's soldiers, forcing them to recede. The Fars army was shaken up, something that never happened before when Haghdar led the army. Haghdar immediately rounded up the army and prepared for the next day of war.

The war continued for six months, and even though Haghdar killed many of the kings, Toufan's soldiers bravely continued the war and killed many of Fars's soldiers. Toufan's soldiers were fighting for their belief and country and not for superiority. Both sides suffered many casualties; neither retreated.

The king of Toufan was injured but continued attending the war and led his army like nothing the Fars army had seen before. He was furious, and his leadership kept Toufan's soldiers buoyant. The Toufan soldiers sensed the rage and vengeance in the king's leadership and continued fighting boldly.

Haghdar sent a message to the king of Fars, explaining the situation; he had killed many kings, each of whom he believed was the real one, yet Toufan's army continued the war. The king of Fars sent a message back, noting that under the circumstances, Haghdar must change his strategy, regroup, and instead of attempting to remove their leadership, eliminate every soldier, officer, and general of Toufan. If it was not possible to identify the true king; he might as well eliminate all of them. His orders were the total annihilation of Toufan's military.

Haghdar ordered his army for an overall attack, and they killed as many of Toufan's soldiers as they confronted. Haghdar, riding Raad, went back and forth quickly, killing everyone on his path and looking particularly for the true king.

On the last day of the seventh month, practically both armies were destroyed. The king himself came to fight Haghdar as all the other great warriors were killed. The fight took seven days, and at the end of the seventh day, Haghdar defeated the king in a one-on-one fight. Haghdar laid the king on the ground, sat on his chest, and removed his hood and that of the king. He asked what his name was.

"The king of Toufan," he said.

Haghdar asked what his father's name was. He said, "The king of Toufan."

Haghdar said, "The king of Toufan, son of the king of Toufan, was killed by the hands of Haghdar, son of Zesht," and pushed his knife into his heart.

He ordered the king to be beheaded and his head sent to the king of Fars in a piece of ragged cloth as he had wished. He then quickly went to the king's palace to take his wife, as was customary then, to prove he took away everything the king had. However, the queen was gone, and there was no knowledge of her whereabouts. Haghdar knew his victory would not be complete without taking the king's wife. The king's soul would be at peace as long as she was safe.

Meanwhile, the army captured the defected generals and brought them to Haghdar. The generals knew the punishment for treachery was death. They bowed before Haghdar and expressed their gratitude. They prayed to the great Haghdar to spare their lives and allow them to go to the farthest point on the planet where nobody would ever hear from them. In return they would show him the hiding place of the queen of Toufan. Haghdar did not accept their offer and ordered one of them to be executed, yet the other two did not confess. They knew their only chance was to cut a deal with Haghdar.

One of the Fars generals suggested torturing the remaining defected generals in order to obtain the desired information. Haghdar responded that Fars did not torture captured enemies, and he would not disgrace the great army of Fars by ignoring traditions. He mentioned the reason for the execution of the general was treason and nothing else. In spite of that, Haghdar knew the generals would not speak even if they were executed unless their request was granted. So he accepted their offer under the condition that he would search for them, and once he found them, he would kill them. The generals accepted his condition and told him the secret hiding place of the queen in a temple guarded by the god of light.

CHAPTER SIXTEEN

THE MEETING

The generals disclosed to Haghdar the location of the temple of the god of light where Shahrara was serving. Haghdar appointed his generals to establish order in Toufan and left to find the queen. He indicated to his generals that it was the order of the king of Fars to start rebuilding Toufan immediately. The king would shortly send funds and support for such a good cause. Then he left to give a visit to the queen of Toufan.

The temple of the god of light was in a remote part of Toufan in a low and vast land surrounded by low plants close to the sea on the west end of the world. To the south, several kilometers before the temple grounds, there were high hills covered with old and tall redwood trees. The waters came inland from the north at the foot of the rocky cliffs, preventing access from north. The current and clouds mostly came from the north and then moved south. To the east, they did not reach far beyond the temple grounds and low plants around it. Further to the east beyond the low plants and thereafter were many kilometers of dead land uninhabitable to most livings. The temple was almost unidentifiable from afar, and unless one was familiar with the settings, it was unnoticed until one reached the grounds around it. The temple was built low too. On the very top of the temple, there was a skylight in the form of an arch. Early at dawn, the very first ray of sunshine rising from beyond the dead land would be cast inside the temple from the east corner of the arched skylight and continued all day shining through. The sun would set into the sea, casting the last ray of the daylight through the west corner of the skylight. On the temple floor right under the arched skylight, there was a large circular platform made of white marble. The ray of sunshine coming through the skylight bounced on the white marble platform, reflecting a rainbow all day. Above the marble platform and under the arched window, the old book of the god of light was placed on a stand. A heliostat was installed right under the skylight above the book of the god of light. It shone sunshine over the Good Book of the god of light and the marble platform all day. The sunshine would cast a shade of the book of the god of light onto the middle of the platform where Shahrara was sitting on the floor, serving her god.

Haghdar arrived at the temple grounds early afternoon and told Raad to stand back. He walked into the temple and came to the place of worship. There, right in the middle of the marble platform, queen Shahrara was sitting on the floor, praying. The beauty of the queen and the reflection of the rainbow on her face was beyond what was said or written about her. He had never seen such beauty, innocence, and peace all at the same time, all in one place. Haghdar looked at her and felt something very strong yet fragile inside. He had conquered many lands and killed many kings and great warriors but never felt the way he did then—fragile and fearful. For the first time in his life, he felt fear—fear of a power entirely different that could surpass his own. He could not talk nor move and was being absorbed in the majestic power of her presence. He did not realize how long he was standing there quietly watching the queen meditating and resolving in the will of the god of light. The day was old and night cast darkness upon the temple when he came to himself.

The queen did not move but was aware of his presence. She knew the tradition but did not know what Haghdar had in mind. She secretly was holding a knife under her gown, ready to push it into her heart if Haghdar came closer. It must have been hours that they were staring at each other without saying a single word. Haghdar eventually extended his right hand to help the queen stand up. Yet Shahrara did not make a move. Haghdar, in a warm and charming voice, asked the queen to stand up. He said he did not have any intention to harm her. The queen said she knew the tradition, and he would not take her alive. Haghdar, with the same tone, replied he did not wish to take her if she did not want to. Haghdar continued that traditions were made and then replaced by gods. And it was time for her to replace the tradition now and forever. Haghdar did not enter the sacred stand and waited for the queen to step out. Shahrara asked then what was it that he wanted. Haghdar said that up to the moment he saw her, the tradition, but thereafter he was not sure. It was the first time Haghdar was not sure and did not know what to do. Haghdar said many lives were lost in the war from both sides, and it was time for healing. Accordingly, he had ordered his army to immediately start rebuilding Toufan, to include Toufanians as citizens of Fars with equal rights, and beginning that moment, only those who raised arms against Fars, assassins, and those who committed treason or broke the laws of the land would be punished according to the Fars and Toufan laws. He continued that those laws of Toufan that were not in conflict with the laws of Fars would be incorporated into the laws of Fars and applied equitably to all the citizens of Fars and Toufan. He declared that the king of Fars wished to disperse freedom, justice, and wealth to the people of Toufan. Fars would expend as much resources and support as required to achieve this righteous and profound purpose. He proclaimed that he and the king of Fars had this vision to create one world in which there was no hunger and no war and all citizens had the right to freedom, justice, and the pursuit of happiness.

Haghdar said that to attain his vision, he needed the wisdom and help of the queen. Together they could make right what had been wrong for both great nations, and it was her responsibility to help with the rebuilding of the greatness of Toufan to remain for the eternity of time. Haghdar stated he always thought his legacy would not be written for the wars he won but for understanding the sufferings of those whom he defeated.

Shahrara replied, "You wagered a war against my country, killed my king, my husband, and my relatives and friends, occupied my beloved land, and now ask for my help. How can I trust you?"

Haghdar responded that he did not come to kill her king, husband, relatives, and friends. He came to fight great warriors because he had a greater vision, one that unified the two great nations as one, where people enjoyed freedom and better lives without fear of war, one that would include the farthest points of the world, one that would raise the quality of the lives of human beings for the unforeseeable future. History would be written about this new nation as the land of opportunity, freedom, justice, fairness, and happiness to all. The unity of these two nations would mark the victory of the god of light over the gods of darkness, disease, and Ahreman. He stated that he did not know much about Shahrara except that she was beautiful, yet even if he did, he would have done the same because his doing was not against one man but was for the good of all. He expressed that he never had any doubt about his ideals, and he would give his life to achieve those humane principles.

Shahrara knew of Haghdar, that he was the greatest warrior, just and wise, but now she met a man with a vision greater than any one nation or land, even Fars. She was not sure what to do. She slowly stood up to step off the marble platform, still holding the knife strong in her hands under her gown. Haghdar softly, and with warm hands that would put a child to sleep, helped her out.

It was almost dawn, and the light was soon coming back through the arched window. They walked about the temple to the dining area. Shahrara said he must be hungry. She prepared some food, and they ate together. Haghdar said he needed some rest. He thought he needed to be alone to think it through. Shahrara directed him to a bedroom and left him a bowl of water and clean towels so he could freshen up. The water in the bowl was clearer than dunes, and the towels had the smell of heaven. He wanted to go back to Shahrara to just be with her. He thought this could not be, yet he could not stop thinking about her. He felt weak and strong at the same time. He then went to bed, trying to put himself to sleep. After a while, he fell asleep and dreamed of Shahrara.

Shahrara realized Haghdar was sleeping and thought it was her chance to take revenge for what he had done to Toufan. She squeezed the knife in her hand and came upon Haghdar as quietly as the reflection of the light. He was in a sound sleep and did not wake up. She lifted the knife with both hands above her head to strike Haghdar's heart with all her strength. But at one split second before she lowered the knife, Haghdar opened his eyes. He saw Shahrara upon himself with the knife in her hands above her head, yet he did not make a move and did not say a word. Instead, he slowly closed his eyes again. He stayed still with eyes closed and waited. Shahrara did not know what to do. Here was the man who killed everyone she loved and most importantly occupied her homeland that she loved so much, yet she could not kill him. She knew she could not do it and therefore dropped the knife. She wanted to run away when Haghdar gently took her hand. Haghdar calmly said that he understood her emotions and might deserve to be killed. Let it be known that he would not ever hurt her under any circumstances, and she could take revenge any time she desired to do so. He assured her he would not stop her or defend himself. He expressed that he came here to take her, to prove he conquered Toufan and took away everything her king had, but instead his heart was conquered by emotions he never felt before. Shahrara said Haghdar never turned back on his words. Was the great Haghdar giving his words to her? He answered; Haghdar gave his word with all his heart to Shahrara, queen of Toufan.

Shahrara sat next to Haghdar and took his hand in hers, which were softer than flower petals. She confided that she did not understand her mixed feelings for the first time in her life. Logically, she should despise Haghdar and try to get rid of him, yet she found the greatness of the man in her heart. Haghdar said that she was not alone. He was confused as well and could not understand why he felt the way he did, but he could not resist it, and although he knew this was against tradition, he simply did not care. All he knew was that he wanted her and he wanted her as his wife—not the queen, just his wife. Shahrara accepted under the condition that she would never have to leave Toufan, her homeland.

CHAPTER SEVENTEEN

Joy to All

Haghdar immediately sent a messenger to the king to give him the good news. The messenger came to the palace of the king of Fars with Haghdar's message. Haghdar wrote, after customary greetings, the mission was accomplished, and the two nations of Fars and Toufan were ready to be one indeed. The message continued that as the great king of Fars wished, the people of Toufan were being treated fairly and justly, and the rebuilding of Toufan was already on its way. The rebuilding, he added, needed the king's graciousness and generosity, of which he assured the people of Toufan. It is for this grand moment that he requested permission from the king of kings to wed the queen of Toufan and complete the unity of the two great nations.

The king of kings was greatly pleased with the progress of his plans and the unity of the two proud nations. The king ordered a generous prize to be given to the messenger for the excellent news. He then sent him back to Toufan to inform Haghdar that such a glorious moment required the presiding of the king, and he would personally visit Toufan to assure Toufanians of his justice and generosity. The king of Fars would then declare the unity of Toufan and Fars nations by attending the ceremonial matrimony of Haghdar and his queen, Shahrara.

HAGHDAR

Haghdar received king's message and was increasingly rejoiced to know his favored king was attending his wedding ceremony. Haghdar ordered the generals and court ministers to make the necessary arrangements for the arrival of the king of kings and that no expense might be spared.

The king arrived at Toufan's capital and was greeted by Haghdar and his bride to be. He immediately went to the palace and ordered a reception of the court's subjects, including priests, ministers, and servants. The king was dressed in Toufan's traditional outfit for grand celebrations with the picture of the sun, symbol of the god of light, on his chest. He started walking toward the royal temple on the other side of the palace almost one kilometer away, with Haghdar and Shahrara on either side one step behind him, and the court priests, ministers, and servants behind them. All of Fars and Toufan's high ranks were standing on either side of the king's walkway. Virgin girls poured flowers before the king's footsteps with a humble gesture of servitude. He walked to the temple and climbed the temple's steps to the highest point. He paid his respect to the god of light.

The king then declared, "From now on, the two great nations of Fars and Toufan will be one in land and one in heart. The new great country is called Faraaz (meaning "above all"), land of freedom, opportunity, and justice for all. Faraaz will recognize freedom of religion and speech for all. Citizens of Faraaz are free to worship their gods based on their own rituals. Citizens are free to express their opinions and ideas about any subject matter from social to business to politics. A justice ministry will be established with branches in major cities where all citizens may send their grievances to the king directly. Toufan's rebuilding already started, and it will enjoy the king's utmost generosity. It is the wish of the king for the people of Toufan to live in liberty and with pride at all times. It is a fortunate moment upon the people of Faraaz and hence the unity of the two nations by announcing the matrimonial union of Haghdar and queen Shahrara."

The king desired the festivity to begin right away. Alas, much time and many human lives had been sacrificed to achieve such a glorious moment for the new great nation of Faraaz.

So the ceremony to wed Haghdar and Shahrara began—a perfect time for a perfect cause. All the kings of Fars and Toufan were attending the festivity and presented their gifts to the king of kings, Haghdar, and Shahrara. It was a joyful and compassionate time for all, one which the king and Haghdar had planned for a long time to be completed by the love and devotion of queen Shahrara.

Nevertheless, Haghdar's happiness was not complete because his father, Zesht, could not attend his wedding. He did not feel good and was not able to travel. Zesht was old and had lost much of his strength. Deep inside Haghdar knew his father would not recover from his illness. Zesht was the source of much of Haghdar's strength and wisdom, and he counseled him on matters most important to him and to Fars. Haghdar did not wish to distort Shahrara's happiness of the occasion with the news and therefore did not say anything. He kept quiet throughout the ceremony. Shahrara felt Haghdar was not himself and somewhat preengaged with some mind-menacing issue. She asked him a few times if there was something bothering him; when he answered, he was caught in the magnet of the moment. He felt a cold sensation in the air, which made him shiver for the first time in his life. Shahrara felt Haghdar's sensation and trembled herself.

The celebration continued for seven days and seven nights. At the end of the seventh night, the king of kings told Haghdar he had to go back to Fars; however, Haghdar may remain in Toufan with his bride as Toufan's king and queen. He must make sure the unity of the two great nations was complete with a sense of pride for all and not impaired under any circumstances. The king added the task at hand was equal to, if not more important than, the defeat of the king of Toufan and his marriage to the queen. Haghdar agreed and assured the king that his wish would be served properly.

Upon departure of the king of kings, Haghdar came back to the palace to his queen. He called his generals, high priests, and ministers and announced, "Shahrara shall be the queen of all lands ruled by Haghdar, and his queen shall only bow to the queen of the king of the kings, the king of all Faraaz." They bowed to the queen Shahrara, and the queen bowed to Haghdar, and Haghdar bowed to them.

Haghdar stayed with Shahrara for forty-nine days and forty-nine nights of rejoicing and happiness. They had all the great senses of love for one another, the country, and what they were to accomplish for such great love. Haghdar understood Shahrara's pain for loss of the king of Toufan and therefore was very careful about every word he said and every move he made. He realized all of this was happening too fast, and Shahrara might need some space to adjust to the new situation. Thus, after forty-nine days and forty-nine nights, Haghdar told Shahrara he must travel to the farthest points of Toufan to see through his promise to the king—to secure liberty, opportunity, and justice for all. Shahrara affirmed Haghdar's intentions and told him the rebuilding of Toufan was above all love and encouraged him to take the trip.

While away, Haghdar received a message indicating his father was dying and had asked to see him at once. He had the most important issue to discuss with him before his death. It was a solemn moment since he had to leave Shahrara before even being able to say farewell, yet on the other hand, he must see his dying father. Haghdar sent a message to Shahrara to explain the situation and his reason for leaving without going back to the palace and seeing his newlywed bride one last time before departure. He had to go directly to Fars to visit his dying father for the last time—that was if he arrived promptly.

Haghdar told Raad there was a difficult journey ahead; they had to race to Fars almost nonstop. He needed to see and talk to his father about an important subject matter before he joined eternity. Raad understood and ran faster than the wind to deliver Haghdar to his father in Fars.

CHAPTER EIGHTEEN

THE DEPARTURE

Haghdar arrived at Zesht's residence in the middle of the night and immediately went to see him in his deathbed. Zesht was half-conscious when Haghdar entered the room. Haghdar was submerged in sad emotions to leave Shahrara on one hand and to see his father in death bed on the other.

Zesht told him he knew he did not have much time to live. For that reason, he must tell him about something of the greatest importance. Zesht explained his childhood being raised by Seepar until the age of seven. He continued that Seepar gave him three of its feathers to burn one at a time whenever he was in great need of help, and Seepar's spirit would appear and help him. But fortunately for him, he never had to use any of them, and now he was turning them over to Haghdar. He told him the DNA of Seepar was embedded in him and therefore his son Haghdar; hence, whenever he was in great danger or in need of help, if he burns one of the feathers, the spirit of Seepar would appear to help him. He warned Haghdar not to use the feathers to bring anybody, including Zesht, back from the dead as Seepar did not have such a power. He emphasized to use them wisely and always remember his spirit would be with him through the spirit of Seepar. He then gave Haghdar the box containing Seepar's feathers.

Haghdar was holding Zesht's head in his hand softly and quietly crying for the first time in his life. Zesht said no man should ever see tears of the great Haghdar. He laid his head on the hands of Haghdar and closed his eyes so his soul might fly to the skies to meet with the god of light above the clouds. Haghdar sat there holding Zesht's body tightly, crying all night. He knew something in his heart, mind, and soul departed, leaving a gap that would never be filled again. He knew he lost a part of himself and wanted to fill that hole with his tears and sorrow, but nothing could heal his wound inside.

Heavy winds and rainfall distorted the silence of his solitude all night long as if the skies were weeping with him.

Early in the morning, Haghdar sent a message to the king of kings to inform him of his father's passing. He prayed for forgiveness, not having gone to the court to pay his respects to the king of kings first. He stated his father had only few moments to live, and he had to go to see him immediately. He also requested to see the king to report the progress of events in Toufan and to discuss matters most important to Fars.

The king had his own dilemma. He wanted the court ministers and servants as well as the generals and the army to accept his first son as the prince and therefrom to be crowned after his death. Although, he believed his son did not yet attain necessary and sufficient experience to be a master politician to govern the kingdom and subjects of that size and variety. He had raised his son with utmost care, preparing him for the time he was to be the king. The king's sons attended military school with best of training in war affairs, politics, and education. The king's first son was the best of friends with Haghdar. He turned out to be a king even greater than his father, but that is another story.

The king was certain of Haghdar's friendship and loyalty to himself and his son but, at the same time, knew the turn of events could put the best of friends at odd positions. He often cautioned his son to foresee the progress of events and prevent any situation that may in any way interfere with his friendship and loyalty to Haghdar; alas, the kingdom would not last long without any of them.

The king had frequently shared his thoughts in this regard with his first son. He mentioned no king—past, present, or future—might replace Haghdar. But the empire needed a powerful and wise king to govern and to uphold the kingdom's strength, vast lands, and ethical values. The king knew his son would make a just king who would follow his teachings and measure up to his greatness, if not exceed it, but he felt the timing was not right yet, and time was flying fast.

The king had made some remarks to the court priests, who brought strong faith and belief to the kingdom, and the ministers and the top generals, who were the pillars of the empire, about his succession without mentioning his son. The ministers, high priests, and generals most close to the king discussed the matter between themselves, each having the aspiration to succeed the king, at least partially if not completely, and therefore suggested to the king to organize a council to advise the king's first son on the most important issues of the Faraaz empire. They also suggested for his son to be seated as the head of the council for more transparency over the council's conduct of affairs and, at the same time, to utilize the wisdom, experience, and knowledge of king's most trusted subjects. They indicated some rumors flew around the palace that Haghdar, now the king of Toufan and married to queen Shahrara, was not pleased with the king's son ascent without being counseled, and that was the original reason behind his absence from Fars. They reasoned, to show to the world the unity and full support of Fars's most powerful ministers and generals behind the king and his son, it was best to organize the council and let everyone knew, Haghdar included, that the entire council's loyalty to the king, severally and jointly, was unbreakable. The council would be against any idea contrary to the king's decisions and unanimously gave their allegiance to the king and His Majesty's son.

The king was not pleased with the idea because he knew the council would be very powerful once organized, and his son would not be able to govern the council without losing some power. He knew the most important decisions for the entire Faraaz would be discussed by the council, and after all, the prince would not be able to overrule the council's decision if they unanimously supported certain policies. The king had been hesitant to disregard the suggestion of the high priests, court ministers, and top generals since they had served the kingdom with utmost loyalty. He was struggling to find a suitable solution to his dilemma and at times was preoccupied with the thought of his succession but could not find a logical argument valid enough to convince the supporters of the idea to organize the council against it.

The next day the king received Haghdar's message and thought finally he found the solution to his burden. He immediately sent a message back to Haghdar, expressing his deep condolences and granting his reception request. In fact, he asked Haghdar to come to the court without further delay as the loss of his father was too big a sorrow to be borne by any one person. The king at once called on the high priests, ministers, and top generals who were available to participate in the reception of Haghdar at the courtyard.

Haghdar, however, desired to go back to Toufan. He needed the compassionate and peaceful arms of Shahrara to rest but realized his king, his father figure; his best friend, the prince; and above all, his country needed him. He was ready to make any and all sacrifices to help with the great cause of the Faraaz nation.

Haghdar entered the palace after dawn when the king and his son were sitting on the throne on top of the hall and all other dignitaries were standing on either side as it was customary for such events. They all were waiting for Haghdar's entrance in silence with their heads down.

Haghdar paid his respects to the king, to the prince, and the audience and then started walking toward the throne. The king and his son stood up, walked toward him, and somberly personally welcomed Haghdar home. The king took his hand in his, walked with him to the throne, and asked him to sit on his left side and his son on the right at an equal level.

The king first ordered seven months of mourning to observe the passing of Haghdar's father and summoned all his subjects—the kings, the ministers, and the generals from the four corners of the globe—to assemble the largest funeral ceremony ever seen or heard by anyone in the entire Faraaz empire, one only worthy of the king of kings' close friend. He proclaimed that it was with a heavy heart that he pronounced the moment filled with sadness and sorrow. He continued that the king always considered himself as father figure, past Zesht, to Haghdar, and the loss of his father, the king's close friend, was a tragic loss not to Haghdar alone but also to the king and the people of Faraaz. The king proclaimed that the world would not be the same without Zesht, and it was with pride that the king declared this sad day as a national mourning day for all time.

After the day's ceremony, the king called on Haghdar to join him in private. Haghdar went to the king's quarters, where he was expected by the king and his first son, the prince. Haghdar and the prince grew up together and were best friends. They did the usual playful greetings. The prince said he wanted to personally submit his condolences to Haghdar, and he always felt he was like a son to Zesht. They sat in an informal manner, and the king ordered some food and refreshments. The king said that unfortunately, they had to attend to some important business in this somber and sad day. The king explained to Haghdar the rumors flying around the royalties and what the high priests and court ministers had told him. Haghdar replied that it was nonsense. He would give his life for his king and his country. Haghdar declared the king and his family were his family, and he would not allow any harm to his family. The king was very pleased and asked Haghdar to stay in his quarters in the palace until the necessary arrangements for the crowning of his son as his replacement was complete. Haghdar accepted and then apologized to leave since it had been a few days of nonstop traveling and did not have time to sleep for that long. The king was tired too, and they called it day.

The funeral ceremony continued for a few months. The kings and celebrities came one by one and paid their respects to Zesht, Haghdar, and the king of kings. During the entire ceremony, Haghdar was sitting to the left and the prince to the right of the king at the same level. The king, the prince, and Haghdar left together every afternoon upon finishing the day's affairs of the kingdom and appeared together the very next morning.

Meanwhile, Haghdar received messages from Toufan indicating Shahrara was bearing his first child. He wished to go back to Toufan and attend to her; however, the kingdom and his country needed him. Haghdar was advised by his ministers and top generals in Toufan that Queen Shahrara was doing very well, and aside from his absence, they had nothing to worry about.

After seven months of the funeral ceremony, the king thought it was time to start his plan for succession and to convince the court officials that not only was his son qualified to wear the crown of the prince, but his friendship with Haghdar was stronger than ever, and Haghdar allegiance belonged to the king and the prince and vice versa. The king thought the timing was right for the prince to earn glory with Haghdar by his side and therefore called Haghdar and the prince and asked them to go to the east, where recently some revolt had arisen and inconsistencies in collected taxes were heightening. He also mentioned Haghdar and the prince should pay their respects back to the kings and celebrities who attended Zesht's funeral by visiting them, as traditionally was done. The king suggested to the prince to take his time and stay over the east for as long as necessary. He concluded that Haghdar must have suffered significantly and needed some time away. It was for the good of the prince as well to rule over the east to establish order and to show people he was ready to officially become the prince of all the Faraaz nation.

Haghdar and the prince started their envoy shortly and traveled to the most remote territories of the east. They went hunting together, chased pheasants, wrestled with each other like they did when they were young teenagers, and enjoyed the time at hand. Meanwhile, Haghdar regularly received messages affirming Queen Shahrara was doing very well, and there was nothing to worry about as far as her condition was concerned. The journey took longer and longer and it seemed to never end, and even though Haghdar missed his queen deeply, the joy of his childhood friendship with the prince gradually reduced the pain of losing his father and separation from Shahrara.

In his son's absence, the king wished to inform the court priests, ministers, and top generals of the progress of events in the east, that Haghdar and his son were establishing order in all the revolting territories, and the empire was solid, stable, and prosperous. The king also informed them that upon the return of Haghdar and his son, the issue of his succession would be decided. He emphasized no ruler of Faraaz nation would be able to maintain and extend the empire's prosperity into the future without allegiance of either Haghdar or the prince, and therefore, their opinion was of utmost importance, if not final.

CHAPTER NINETEEN

The Scheme

Back in Toufan, affairs were different. Top generals appointed by Haghdar to govern Toufan in his absence had received rumors about the differences of opinion between Haghdar and the king flying around the royalties. Haghdar was absent for an extended period of time without even once visiting his expecting wife. Moreover, beyond such a long absence, Haghdar and the prince were sent by the king to the east to supposedly establish order in some revolting regions. They believed the mission was not critical enough to require Haghdar and the prince to be commissioned at the same time, and therefore, most likely there were more important reasons behind the mission. They held a meeting and discussed the king of Fars's motives in order to find underlying reasons; a mission for Haghdar and the prince himself, which a lower-ranking general could comfortably accomplish. Haghdar was sent to the east rather than the west, where his expectant queen was. They came to the conclusion that the king did not approve of Haghdar's child to be born and raised in Toufan and therefore did not wish Haghdar to see his child. The king knew about the loyalty and love of Toufan's women for their country. They raised their children with the same loyalty and love of Toufan, if not more. This child, once succeeded Haghdar, would not have sufficient loyalty to the king of Fars. Instead, his loyalty would belong to Toufan—a danger to Fars's throne. Even worse, Queen Shahrara and her son could convince Haghdar to turn against Fars, the greatest threat to the king of kings.

If that was true, the differences of opinion between the king and Haghdar could present an opportunity for the generals, or at least one of them, to replace Haghdar and become the king of Toufan. They did not dare to take any action against the queen and Haghdar individually and hence decided to organize a council, and the council would make decisions regarding this unprecedented finding. The council was organized consisting of three top generals, three highest priests, and three highest ministers, all of whom agreed Haghdar's child must not be born alive. They thought the king would be very pleased if Haghdar's son was naturally dead and might even give them a prize and a promotion and, at the same time, keep Haghdar in the east for an unspecified period of time. The council then summoned Shahrara's personal chef and provoked him to include in her meal certain drug presented by the high priests. They explained the drug would strengthen the queen physically and emotionally and, at the same time, improve health of Haghdar's son. However, they swore the chef to secrecy about the medicine since, otherwise, it might cause the queen to become suspicious without warrant and therefore to refuse taking the medicine. They generously gave the chef gold and other forms of compensation for his services and asked him to regularly report to the high priests all updates regarding this very important matter. The chef grasped the council's scheme but did not say anything and accepted the prize and the mission.

The council regularly received updates from the chef and sent messages to Haghdar, explaining the queen was doing well and the child, predictably a son, was healthy and strong just like Haghdar himself, and assured him they would inform him periodically of the queen and her child's well-being.

Shahrara was growing bigger and bigger, and the high priests predicted she would give birth to a boy, probably as big as Haghdar himself at birth. Her child would be bigger at birth than most one-year-olds. She had gradually lost her mobility and energy and was getting pale and weak. The high priests and court ministers diagnosed her situation resulted from carrying the child, which was not ordinary by any measure. Shahrara felt something was wrong but could not figure it out. She had a feeling she might not live long enough to give birth to her child and hence called on her most trusted servant to plan for the birth of the child. Shahrara told her servant that Haghdar was absent for several months now, and she might not live long enough to give birth to her child. Thus, in case she died and the child was born alive, she must announce that the child was born dead and then secretly take him or her to the farthest place in Toufan and raise the child as her own. Shahrara alleged her life and her child's life was in great danger because the ambitious generals would want to take advantage of Haghdar's absence and eliminate any succession of his descent in order to become the king of Toufan themselves. Shahrara instructed her servant to never tell the child who his or her parents were though to teach him or her about love for Toufan and that, if there was one thing his mother would have wanted, it was that the child love Toufan above all.

Shahrara's condition was worsening daily, and she had lost all hope to survive and to see her child and Haghdar one last time. She instructed her servant to secretly make all necessary arrangements as she was getting closer to the due date. The very night she gave birth to her son, Shahrara lived only a few short minutes to have a glance of him, and then her soul flew to the skies to rest at the presence of the god of light above the clouds.

Upon Shahrara's death and the birth of her son, the servant immediately informed the generals and the high priests of her passing, resulting in giving birth to a dead boy, as instructed by her. She told them it would be best if she buried him in a remote place to conclude Haghdar's succession before he was informed. The generals were very pleased with the servant's suggestion since it would remove the burden of their scheme and shift it to the servant. The servant had made all the necessary arrangements previously and went away at once with the child. She traveled far and wide to the west and started her life with the child incognito.

Haghdar's son was a big and strong boy. The servant adopted him as her own. She named him Zodiak (meaning "water of life"). Zodiak showed an impressive interest in horseback riding, archery, hunting, and wrestling, among other sports and physical activities. The servant did not tell him about his mother and father, and Zodiak considered her as his mother. As a child, Zodiak sometimes asked about his father. She responded that his father was a warrior who spent all his life in war affairs and whose whereabouts was unknown. Zodiak was wary of his father since he never visited and therefore must have disliked him even before birth. Early in his life, Zodiak decided that someday he would find his father, although he had mixed feelings about him.

CHAPTER TWENTY

LIES THAT FLY

Upon the assumed death of Shahrara and her son, the council held a meeting to plan a strategy to inform Haghdar of the sad news. They decided to announce seven days of mourning for the death of the queen and her son, a funeral deserved by a queen, and immediately sent a messenger to Haghdar. The messenger went to the east and requested permission to see Haghdar since he had important news to report. Haghdar admitted the messenger. He first paid his respects and stated that unfortunately, he carried very sad news and expected to be executed for bringing such news to the great Haghdar. Haghdar felt his heart drop and could not speak. The messenger said it was with grave sorrow that he must inform the great Haghdar his queen and son were dead at his son's birth because the newborn was too big and Queen Shahrara could not support him. The innocent child was dead long before birth, and then the queen died upon delivering the dead newborn.

Haghdar told the messenger he might leave; however, if he ever saw him again, he would kill him with his own hands. The messenger paid his gratitude to Haghdar for his graciousness and left at once.

Haghdar felt great sorrow upon receiving the sad news but could not believe it since he had received frequent messages that Shahrara and his son were doing just fine. He was in a state of denial for few days before he finally started to think rationally. The messenger's explanation appeared reasonable since his own mother died before delivering him. The cause of her death was also said to have been Haghdar's size. He thought, within a few months, he had lost his father, his wife, and his son before he was ever born. Haghdar felt doubts in his heart about the path he had chosen. He thought that maybe if he had stayed with Shahrara, he could have saved her, maybe with the help of Seepar. He cried days and nights quietly, hearing his father saying no man should ever see the great Haghdar's tears. He was not ashamed of crying, but he cared about all the people who put their faith in him. Their entire faith was built on his strength to face difficult times and to come out of them triumphantly. If he broke down, the entire Faraaz would fall, and his beloved country would be conquered by savages and barbarians. His strong and faithful army would be defeated, men killed, and women and children taken as slaves. The entire fate of the human beings and the civilization he had worked so hard to build could take a setback for thousands of years to come. He knew he could not allow his misery to destroy a kingdom as just and vast as Faraaz. He knew he would never again live an ordinary man's life, and from that point, his entire life would be devoted to the ideas by which Faraaz was founded—the pillars of a free, happy, and strong nation where justice was served to all citizens and where humans' color of skin, beliefs and practices, gender, ethnicity, and social class would not prevent anybody from achieving his or her goals.

Haghdar sat in his majestic chair for long periods and, for the first time, thought about his life. He never saw his mother, whom he was told was a servant of the god of light. He did not see his father until the age of ten. His father passed before he was twenty-four, and his wife, the only woman he ever truly loved, died shortly after they met. And his son, whom he never saw, died before birth. There was no logical reason, it seemed, yet he knew there was more to his life. Even though puzzled by the recent events, he prayed to the god of light not to make it harder than he felt then. He thought, on one hand, he had accomplished this practically impossible and likely improbable mission to unite the world and extend justice and freedom to all. On the other, he had a personal life full of painful sequence of events, all of which were beneficial to the human race for thousands of years to come yet at the cost of deep suffering inside.

Some other time, he thought the god of light chose Haghdar to solely serve him and its purpose and nothing else. Yes, that was the reason for the path the god of light had bestowed upon him. Haghdar had mixed feelings about everything he ever believed in. But he knew that either he had to choose his path to the future, or it would be chosen for him, right or wrong. He thought of burning one of Seepar's feathers his father had given him but remembered Seepar did not have the power to bring back anyone from dead. At times he thought there was nothing worth fighting for; then again, he could not deny the happiness and wealth he brought to his people. He just could not let them down.

All these thoughts and feelings were passing through his mind with the speed of light. He knew that not before long, there would come a time for him to make his decision. These thoughts gradually deteriorated his strength and self-esteem.

Haghdar was in despair and did not wish to see anybody, not even the prince, his best friend. He did not eat for days nor go out of his quarters for weeks and announced no visitors, including the prince.

The prince received the report of the sad news for Haghdar but wanted to wait until Haghdar was ready to see him. He knew he needed solitude. He immediately informed the king, and the king announced yet another seven months of mourning for the passing of the queen of Toufan and her son.

The prince stayed around all this time and prayed to the god of light for the healing of Haghdar. The prince sent a message to Haghdar to express his deepest sorrow and condolences and that, at any time he needed his friend, to just call on him. Even though Haghdar and the prince did not see each other for months, they both felt their friendship was getting stronger. They bonded through the silent sadness of the occasion.

CHAPTER TWENTY-ONE

THE ESCAPE

The two generals who directed Haghdar to the temple of the god of light where Shahrara was hiding ran away immediately after he freed them. They knew Haghdar never went back on his words, and as promised, he would find them and then would kill them with his own hands. They could not go to the east toward Fars because they would be arrested shortly and delivered to Haghdar. To the west, there were high seas and what was called the Seas of No Return. The north was cold, and they would freeze to death as they traveled farther and farther, so they decided to go south. They participated in the war against the savages by the Sea of Fars and were hoping to find refuge deep south.

They passed the Sea of Fars and then eastward to nowhere land. The generals, in their journey, were seeking some leverage, anything to either secure their safety or to prevent Haghdar from looking for them. They heard about a priest who was the king of Mantik many years ago and his fight with Seepar, and even though he lost his country, he obtained some supernatural powers with which he forced the king of Fars to proclaim his temple as an independent sovereign living place where he would be free of all doings on the grounds of his temple. All living on the temple grounds would be subject to the king's proclamation. They concluded the temple would be the only place Haghdar could not enter without the priest's permission. So they traveled at night and in disguise toward the east and way downward south. They traveled many months and came to the temple where the ex-king of Mantik was the high priest.

The temple's subjects were mostly individuals escaping from the law. Some of those rulers who did not pledge their loyalty to the king of Fars after he conquered Mantik were among the temple's subjects. As the price for living in the temple, they surrendered to the high priest a handwritten correspondence from the king of Toufan they had held dear for many years. The priest thought that somewhere, somehow the handwritten letter by a king should benefit him, although, at the time, he did not know how.

The temple's subjects knew the temple was their final and only refuge as long as the priest lived. The king's proclamation declared clemency for the priest, and all lived in the temple for as long as he lived. They knew upon his death, the king would take over the temple and destroy it as the symbol of the gods of darkness. He would have everybody arrested and prosecuted. Upon conviction, they generally expected to be executed in order for the king to put an end to their remnants. Naturally, they did everything within their abilities to keep the high priest healthy and hopeful because their own lives depended on his livelihood.

The generals arrived at the temple and appeared before the high priest. The high priest asked them why they went to him. They explained their life story and tendered their loyalty to the priest only if he allowed them to stay in the temple. They said they had fought for the Fars army and were generals themselves. They claimed they could train the high priest's subjects to become professional soldiers instead of small-time thieves and thugs.

The high priest still had his ambition of killing Seepar and thereafter ruling the world. He thought that even though the generals were not the ones to help him kill Seepar, they could be a starting point. He paused for a few seconds and then told them the temple was a small place, and already there were too many people living in it. There was not enough food or shelter for everyone, and they needed them more than military training. Besides, no matter how trained the soldiers became, they would be arrested or killed as soon as they set foot outside the temple. The high priest continued that no matter how skilled they became, they were no match for the military power of Fars and especially Haghdar. The generals replied that it was true that no ordinary army could defeat Fars, but with the help of certain forces at hand, Fars may be defeated and Haghdar killed. They noted that the first fight would be against Seepar and not Fars. They must train and be ready for the right day to climb the highest mountain and reach Seepar and kill it. The high priest was interested and asked them what they knew about Seepar. They said that in their journeys to the south and underworld, they learned about a certain myth that said there would be a young boy who would kill Seepar and then raise an army to defeat all and conquer the world, even Fars. They said they did not know who this boy was, but if the high priest had a well-trained army, he could join the boy, and with his wisdom and the generals at his side, he could become the ruler of the world. The boy would be to him what Haghdar was to the king of Fars.

The high priest smiled and told them they might stay, only as long as they trained the outlaws and made soldiers out of them. The generals agreed and started their work in the temple. They rounded up all the young men living in the temple grounds and promised them victory if they worked hard and did exactly as instructed. The generals worked day and night and not only trained outlaws to become soldiers but also taught them to manufacture artillery. They started to build a small yet very efficient squad, one that could fight against all odds. The soldiers were trained to be merciless and ferocious, who enjoyed destruction more than conquering. The small army started to grow as more and more outlaws heard about their activities. They joined them to the extent that the temple grounds could not house any more of them.

It was a few years since the generals came to the temple. The generals and their squad of highly trained soldiers were eagerly anticipating the promised boy who would supposedly kill Seepar to show up any time. They looked for any sign to display them the light for the identification of this miracle boy.

The high priest was anxious himself to meet this boy. He had lost his three sons, his kingdom, and its wealth following his dream.

He thought he had paid his dues and it was time for him to rise to glory. The miracle boy was his savior. He had to be very careful this time as there was no room for error. And many days and nights passed, but no indication of the miracle boy was in sight.

CHAPTER TWENTY-TWO

OH, BOY

Zodiak was no ordinary child. He was big and strong and grew fast since birth not only physically but also mentally and spiritually. As an infant, he would go swimming in the sea all day and into the middle of the night. His fearlessness was unique and unmatched. Early on he became the leader of the neighborhood's children, some as old as three times his age. These children would come to him for help with their homework and any other issue they had. He was like a big brother to them and helped them any way he could. He developed fast and learned faster. He could read and write by the age of two. He spent most of his time either studying or exercising. He read stories about the great Haghdar and the wars he won and dreamed to be like him when he grew up. He read all he could about war strategies and tactics employed by the great Haghdar and wanted to go to Fars and join its army as soon as possible, just like Haghdar did, but his mother warned him against it every time.

Other than his mother, Zodiak did not have any family member; he respected his mother's advice. She told him there were dark forces against him and his existence, and therefore, he must live anonymously until the right time came. His life was endangered by these forces of the gods of darkness who tried to kill him before birth. He asked his mother about the reason for these forces wanting him dead. He had never hurt anyone. In fact, even though he was just a child, he helped many others. He argued someday these forces would find him, and he would have to confront them. He believed hiding and living in fear was not the answer. But his mother said he was too young to understand the sequence of events starting before he was conceived and continuing to this day and on to the future. He must believe her, and when the right time came, she would disclose the truth to him. Meanwhile, she asked him to keep up his work to acquire knowledge, do well with his studying, and exercise since confronting the servants of the gods of darkness required the strength of a hundred warriors and the wisdom of a hundred kings.

Zodiak continued his work as advised by his mother and became wiser and stronger by the day though always wondered who his father was. What kind of a man was he? Was he still alive at all, and if he was, what did he do? Maybe he was killed in one of those wars and never heard of again. In any case, he was determined to either find him or to find out about him. Dead or alive, he wanted to know who his father was and why he never visited or contacted him. Not only did he never visit or send a message, he also refused to help him to fight against these forces who wanted to eliminate him from the face of the planet. At times he thought maybe the reason he must live incognito was that his father was one of the servants of the gods of darkness. He must not know Zodiak was alive or else he would come to kill him, yet something inside told him there must be more to his life than just being the son of a servant of the gods of darkness. He felt more and more drawn to the idea of traveling around the world to find his father.

When he was only seven years old, he told his mother he wished to travel and see the rest of the world. Their place of living was remote and boring. It was a little village by the sea visited only by few sailors occasionally stopping at the village's small harbor only to bring food and other supplies. Sailors were the only means of communication Zodiak had with outside world. As a child, he asked them to bring books and other information about other places, big cities, the king, and especially about Haghdar. Other than that, nothing really happened there. He had read all the books existed in that region. He needed to fly away and find his place in the world, but his mother warned him again and again against the forces of Ahreman and implored him to stay.

Zodiak accepted his mother's advice and continued his work. He was a great horse rider, among other activities. He could hop on and off his horse like a stone bouncing off the water. He also enjoyed archery especially on the back of a horse. Other than wild nature and waters, horses were the only valuable product of his living place. He had this urge to travel around the world and, at the same time, look for his father, but he loved his mother and did not wish to do anything without her approval.

As Zodiak grew bigger and stronger, keeping up with him was becoming harder and harder for his mother. She was gradually getting old and losing her strength. When Zodiak was ten years old, she became very sick and lost all her energy. The neighborhood priest told him she did not have much more time to live. He asked him how much more time she had. He responded maybe few days at most.

On the day she was dying, Zodiak sat next to his mother in their small hut. He could not stop staring at her and weeping. He exclaimed she was the only person he ever had and loved in his short life. He did not think it was fair that she would pass. She was a good person and an excellent mother to him.

She said there was something she had to tell him as she could not meet the god of light after death with the heavy weight of the secrets she carried. She explained his real mother was Shahrara, queen of Toufan, who was poisoned and killed by certain Fars generals. The same forces attempted to kill him before birth.

Shahrara descended from kings for hundreds of years, and some believed she descended from the gods. She was actually Shahrara's faithful servant. She was most trusted by her. Shahrara asked her to take him to a faraway place where nobody could find him. That was the reason she escaped and brought him to this nowhere land. She said she told the Fars's generals Zodiak was dead at birth to prevent them from searching for him. Shahrara wanted her to never tell anybody about this fact but must know that he had the marks of the god of light. He would make it great one day if he stayed alive as these forces of darkness would not have mercy on him. He was to become the king of Toufan, and that was not acceptable to those Fars generals. They had planned to become king themselves. Zodiak asked who these generals were. She said they were the commissioned council by the king of Fars to rule Toufan. He asked about his father. She said, "Your father was the . . ."—she had a hiccup—"the . . ."

But she could not finish her sentence and passed before telling him the name of his father. Zodiak sat there and wept all night. He thought, not only he did not have anybody in this world who cared for him, but the forces of the gods of darkness sought to kill him. A child only ten years old had to confront the agents of the gods of darkness. He felt alone and insecure. What was he to do? Where was he to go, and more importantly how could he stay away from those who wanted to see him dead? He did not have anybody in the entire world to rely on and to protect and shelter him. He would never again feel love, sincere love like that of his mother.

The next day, he buried his mother and then gathered as much wood as he could. He waited for the darkness of the night. In the middle of the night, he set the ragged hut of his living place on fire and started his journey to find his father. He was determined to search for and find these Fars generals someday and take revenge against them. It was not a choice for him. If he did not destroy these forces of the gods of darkness, they would find and destroy him. He knew he had to exercise caution and wait until the right moment came. These generals were powerful and merciless.

Zodiak went to the harbor and started working in a ship as a crew moving goods to other villages near the shore. He stayed away from his home village and wished the people there to forget about him. He traveled to many different places, always looking for any information to lead him to his father. He presumed his father must have known these generals who wanted to kill him. Gradually and as the time passed, the seeds of vengeance grew bigger and bigger inside him. He worked hard in ships at a young age, cleaning and carrying goods on his shoulders. He grew stronger and wiser as time passed. He soon learned sailing, became the ship's skipper, and traveled farther and farther. Because of the affluence of the east, he decided to travel farther to the east and bring goods and commodities to the west. He had to travel longer distances and the work was harder, but he made more money and the ship owners were pleased with his performance. As he traveled farther to the east, he learned about the king of Mantik, now a priest, his temple, and the two generals living on his temple grounds. He learned they were refugees from the king of Fars and thought they must have valuable information about his father. They might even be the generals who killed his biological mother or have knowledge about those agents of darkness who wanted to see him dead. At any rate, they could be a clue to his past, his parents, and his enemies.

So he decided to go to Mantik and meet with these generals. Zodiak was fourteen years old when he came to the temple in northern Mantik. The priest was astounded by his size and strength but did not make any gesture. He asked him why he went there. Zodiak said he had heard the priest once was the king of Mantik but lost his kingdom to the king of Fars. He continued that he also lost something of immense value to the king of Fars and wished to return the favor.

Zodiak said he knew the priest trained a small army for years on the temple grounds under the supervision of two of Fars's refugee generals, but his army needed a leader as strong and as wise as Haghdar to defeat the king of Fars. The priest was interested; he concealed his smile and inquired if Zodiak believed he was that man. Zodiak said he would be with the help of the priest and his army, but in return, he must be assured that the lives of certain generals of Fars belonged to him. He knew they existed but did not know yet who they were, only that they were commissioned by the king of Fars to rule Toufan. He concluded he had every intention to look them up and, upon finding them, to kill them.

The priest's heart was illuminated by the words he was hearing, and rays of hope shone on his soul. The priest paused momentarily then said he was an old man and had only one wish, to become the king of Fars before he died. He did not care about any of Fars's generals except the two who were his subjects. Zodiak could kill any general or, even better, the king himself as long as he became king.

He promised, upon victory over Fars's fiendish army, Zodiak would be to him what Haghdar was to the king of Fars. He affirmed his sons were dead, he had no other living relative, and upon conquering Fars, he would make Zodiak his first prince to only become king after his death. He claimed he knew just how to defeat Fars, only if Zodiak was the promised boy, even though the chances were slim and danger grave. But first, Zodiak had to prove to him he was the man for the job. Zodiak smiled for the first time ever since his mother died.

Zodiak inquired from the generals their reason for seeking refuge in the temple if in fact they were generals. They told him Haghdar wanted to kill them because they were good to the people of Toufan. They married Toufanian women and loved the land. Alas, Haghdar's never-ending hatred for Toufan was evidenced by the destruction and death he brought to it, and then he left without ever returning. He promised wealth and freedom to Toufanians but delivered death and obliteration. Zodiak said "Revenge is the work of fools, but if you have to take it, you must be prepared to risk everything", and left it at that.

Zodiak joined the priest's small army immediately. He soon realized that although they were well trained, they never went outside the temple and never participated in a real fight. He was by far better than any of those warriors and soon became their leader. After three months, he told the priest his small army must start some activities outside the temple to measure their strength and abilities in the real world. The priest was not certain it was the time. He told Zodiak that in case the king of Fars learned he went outside the temple and he would find out, his clemency would be waived and the Fars army would come to the temple to arrest and then kill him and everybody else living on the temple grounds. Zodiak smiled and replied that as long as he was afraid of the king of Fars, he would not get out of the temple, which was exactly what the king wished. Zodiak sarcastically asked how in the world the priest reckoned to defeat the king of Fars and rule the world if he was afraid of him to the point of not even daring to leave the temple grounds.

Zodiak explained they would go out at night and to the other side of the mountain to fight a few of Fars's soldiers. They would not know where they came from and would not know who they were. The priest accepted yet secretly made the necessary arrangements to make a run in case Zodiak was captured or killed by Fars soldiers. He made plans to escape to the south and join some outlaws beyond the Sea of Fars in case Zodiak did not come back by the break of dawn following the night of the mission.

Zodiak rounded up some twenty of the best warriors in the temple. One dark night, when the moon was covered with clouds, they ran around the foot of the mountain and came to the other side of it. Then they approached a small army post where Fars soldiers were relaxing since there had not been any disorder for an extended period. Zodiak accounted for some ten soldiers outside and another maybe fifty inside the army structure. He commanded his warriors to quietly kill the soldiers outside using their bows and arrows. He shot four of them with lightning speed. Then they entered the building. The soldiers immediately picked up their weapons to fight back, but it was too late. Zodiak moved like the wind, and his sword cut the soldiers' necks with every strike. They killed all soldiers in a matter of few minutes, collected weapons, food, and valuables, and left the place before anybody saw them. They headed straight back to the temple.

Zodiak went directly to the priest and explained their expedition and subsequent success over Fars soldiers. He said Fars's army would shortly discover their casualties and next time would be ready for them. He guessed that probably some investigators would be dispatched to survey the incident before the military police interfered. That would give them some time to make preparations for the next phase of their plan, which was to defeat and destroy such an envoy. But thereafter, Fars would send the army to deal with them. Zodiak inquired from the priest to reveal his knowledge and powers to him before they had to confront the Fars army. The priest was hesitant and at first refused to confide his knowledge of Seepar but then realized the journey had already begun and there was no turning back. The priest explained his encounter with Seepar and that only the person who killed Seepar and washed himself in its blood would be able to defeat Fars. The priest said Seepar had superpowers and would absorb the strength and wisdom of its preys. Many men took their chances, and he was the only one who came back alive after having lost his three sons and subsequently his throne.

The priest told him Seepar lived above the highest mountain on top of a flat rock. There were three ways to get to Seepar's nest. One was by flying, the other was to crawl under the flat solid rock horizontally and then to go to the edge of it and climb over, and the third was from behind, where there was a steep fall deeper than the darkest point of hell. No man had ever been able to explore the bottom of the fall. It was said that Ahreman lived there. All in all, the three ways were impossible to pass. He then explained his encounter with Seepar and how he tricked it to come down from its nest on top of the bedrock to consume his son and the fight that took place. But even though Seepar had not consumed any man in a hundred years, it was able to kill and eat all his three sons and thereupon would maintain its strength and powers for another three hundred years. Zodiak asked that once a man reached on top of the deck where Seepar lived, how might he kill it and wash himself in its blood? The priest replied that would be the most difficult part of the mission. He would have to carry Seepar to the edge of the deck, put its head at the very edge, jump up, and on his way down, chop off its head and let its blood pour down like a waterfall and immediately go under it in order to wash himself in its showering blood. The priest stated he figured that was impossible to be accomplished by any mortal, yet there had to be one who could finish the job. In conclusion, as much as he would love to accompany him, the priest asserted, he was too old to take the journey, and Zodiak must go alone.

Zodiak smiled bitterly and conferred this was not the job for an army or warriors; this was the job for one man meeting his destiny. Zodiak told the priest he would leave soon to meet with Seepar, and upon return, they could start their campaign against Fars. The priest agreed. Zodiak then suggested that the generals were capable of doing missions around the temple. The priest nodded in confirmation and added that Zodiak had to concentrate on his journey and the critical mission ahead.

The priest, being weary of the Fars soldiers' death, thought Zodiak's departure would give him a befitting excuse just in case the Fars army investigated the incident. He would simply blame Zodiak for the killing of the soldiers.

The priest gave him his blessings and insisted Zodiak not to take the path of the cliffs as he would be dead before he started his journey. Early the next morning, before the first ray of sunshine, Zodiak started his voyage toward Seepar's place of living.

CHAPTER TWENTY-THREE

LIFE AFTER DEATH

After Haghdar learned about Shahrara's passing, he became impatient, irritated, and filled with sorrow for a few months. The prince had sent him several messages to console him but did not receive a response to any of them. He knew Haghdar was in despair and wanted to help him, but Haghdar had confined himself in his melancholic sensation of losing the one and only love of his life and was not willing to share his pain with anybody else. In fact, he was not willing to share anything with anybody any longer. In his distorted imagination, he envisioned himself being with Shahrara and fancied the moment he saw her until he left more than a hundred times. He clung to Shahrara's memory and did not want to let go.

The prince sent a message to the king and informed him of Haghdar's condition. He explained he could not reach him for the first time since they met, and that was the biggest problem. Haghdar was lost in a sea of sadness and regression for what he had convinced himself of neglecting to do. His grief for leaving Shahrara and especially not being with her when she needed him the most led him to believe it was his fault. He could not relieve himself of the guilt he felt. As the time passed, the guilt feeling affected him deeper and deeper, to the point that he screamed in sleep at night and woke up in cold sweat. He had nightmares of being with her, and then suddenly a nine-headed snake would break out from under his skin and swallow her and then turn around and bit him so painfully that he woke up screaming in pain. On other nights, he had nightmares of playing with his son, his face covered with thick colors of darkness, then some Ahreman walked out of the middle of an intense mist and gave him a knife with which he poked his son's eye, but then he realized it was his own heart he ripped.

Haghdar had lost a tremendous amount of weight, and his skin was pale, his arms weak, and his back bowed. A few most trusted servants who were allowed to go into Haghdar's quarters said he was to die shortly if he continued to treat himself like he did. The king, prince, servants, army, and entire country was sad, worried, and inflicted with hopelessness because of Haghdar's condition. Their hero, the greatest warrior and most admired person in thousands of years, the backbone of the Faraaz nation and kingdom, and the faith of humanity was in jeopardy, and seemingly, there was nothing anybody could do to remedy his impediment.

Haghdar did not even visit Raad, his most trusted general. He, at times, thought of it but then again became careless since he was not in any condition to ride Raad. He occasionally decided to release Raad and let it go back to its original abode but always postponed it to the next day, maybe next week, or next month. Raad was free anyway and could leave anytime it wanted. Most likely it had already left, he thought. He was not ready to be concerned with anybody or anything else other than his guilt, sorrow, and the unfortunate death of Shahrara and his son.

The king of kings had received reports that there were scattered revolts and riots in many parts of the Faraaz empire. In the east, in particular, some outlaws had attacked an army post at night and killed all the soldiers stationed there. Other information reflected that the previous king of Mantik had raised a small yet well-trained army seemingly to fend off robberies from his temple but secretly gaining power and might have had some hand in the killing of the soldiers. Many territories were behind their taxes, and there existed inaccuracies in those collected.

To the west, the council consisted of top generals, high priests, and court ministers commissioned to rule Toufan until the return of Haghdar did not send regular reports of their income and overall updates of the affairs of Toufan. They, more or less, had ceased communication with the king. They once reasoned to the king that the people of Toufan had learned about Haghdar's condition, even some rumors that he was killed by a boy in some eastern army post, and therefore refused to obey the laws and their governance. They had asked for some reinforcements in the form of funds and additional troops to establish and maintain order, but the king was more concerned about the state of Fars rather than Toufan and disregarded their requests. The generals basically stated they were doing the best they could, and without the king's help and wisdom, no improvement could be expected.

Further, Toufan warriors deserted the army and created their own territories. Many wars, in smaller scales, were in progress between these warriors over power, land, wealth, women, and horses.

In Fars, there were riots and an uprising by those who had mostly lost their wealth and believed the king was not able to control the downward spiral of the economy any longer. Social unrest was reported in many different parts of the country.

Even in his court, high priests, generals, and ministers were pressuring the king to organize the council as they had suggested previously, except this time to be headed by the king himself, to reform the army absent of Haghdar, and to bring order and the rule of law to the country. Nobody talked about the prince anymore as it seemed he was out of the picture with Haghdar lost in nightmares and confusion. Disbelief and disappointment was replacing hope and strength. Insecurity and corruption was creeping into the souls and minds of Faraaz nation. The strongest and most ambitious agents of the gods of darkness were advancing in an accelerating pace, casting the fearsome shame of the darkness upon Faraaz and, in particular, Fars.

The country's wealth was gradually depleting, and despite the king's utmost attempts to cure this ill path to misery, the Faraaz nation and the Fars kingdom were falling apart with increasing speed as the time passed. It was becoming apparent in and out of the king's court that nothing could fill the gap of power caused by the absence of Haghdar except for those mis-fortune powerful agents of the darkness.

Haghdar stayed in the east and promised himself to never go back to Toufan again. Years passed, and there was no indication of improvement in Haghdar's condition. Hope was deteriorating, and the Faraaz nation lost its grip on power to the point that many smaller kings declared independence and refused to obey the laws of Fars and the ruling of the king of kings. The king raised an army and led them to fights around the country, but there were too many smaller kings, and some of them were gaining power by defeating other smaller kings. These kings ignored the king of Fars's ruling completely, and some claimed that if and when it would come to war against Fars, they would be victorious, but none of them dared to go beyond talk; no king dared to raise arms in an all-out war against the king of Fars yet, but the inevitable was becoming more and more evident.

The king was desperate and finally decided to meet with Haghdar personally whether he agreed or not. He thought he could not give up his country and his humane vision to which he had devoted his entire life. He therefore must make one final attempt to talk to Haghdar like the loving father he was to him. Thus, he went to the east and directly to Haghdar's quarters unannounced one morning. Haghdar was thin and weak; the king hardly recognized him. Tears came to the eyes of the king, seeing Haghdar reduced to a miserable peasant. He took Haghdar's hand in his, just like he did after the passing of Haghdar's father. He sat next to him and put his arm around his thin shoulders and let him put his head on his shoulder and cry. The king cried with him too and shared his immense sadness. The king's sadness was more profound since he almost lost all hopes for the revival of Fars, seeing Haghdar in that condition. After a while, the king wiped his tears and said he understood Haghdar's despair and was there to stay for as long as necessary. He said he felt Haghdar's loss with his soul and flesh, but there were other losses in progress that were equally grave. He asked Haghdar what the greatest love was that he carried in his heart before meeting Shahrara. Haghdar said it was the love of his country and his king. The king continued that he was extremely desolate because of the regrettable perishing of Shahrara and his son, but Fars and the Faraaz nation still might be salvaged. There was still a slim, very slim chance to save Fars, but it required devotion and sacrifices of an enormous magnitude by everyone, including the king, Haghdar, the prince, and all else. The path was clear—either let go of his biggest love in existence and hence lose all on top of his loss of Shahrara, or make a stand and save what was left of the country, what was left of his love, and what was left of the kingdom. His refusal to face reality would not only result in the loss of Fars but would tarnish the Fars kingdom, the vision they both worked for their entire lives and their legacy for the eternity of time. Fars was on its track of being defeated and the king, the prince, and Haghdar killed or taken as slaves. The future of humanity, the prevalence of the god of light, and all that was good were in jeopardy.

The king asked, What says the great Haghdar? What path would he take, and what would he wish history to write about his legacy? Haghdar lifted his head and looked directly into the king's eyes, full of tears. He saw through the king's eyes his love for Fars and its well-being. The king's words pierced the walls of solitude he had created around himself for all this time and touched his heart. The king was right. There still existed the love of country, which he could not and neither should allow to die. He stood up and walked around the room for a while. He could not find the words to express his regret for the lost time. He finally stated that the king's wisdom reigned above all. The king's sincerity and high morals had always guided him to choose the right path, and this time was no exception. He declared, from that point thereafter, he would devote every second of his life to the goodness of the Fars kingdom. He was lost for almost a decade, but not anymore. He promised with his life to make right what went wrong. The king smiled and said, "This is the Haghdar I knew." I knew Haghdar would not turn his back on his country no matter how deep of a sorrow he felt. Together they would bring the glory and honor back to the Faraaz nation for an infinite time. Haghdar announced that a new day had begun, and he wished to start his renewed mission in life immediately. Haghdar requested from the king to give him some time to get back into shape. He would regularly report to the king of kings of the progress of his condition and would go to the court as soon as he was ready. The king said he must attend some business before the return of Haghdar to the palace, and therefore, this would be an excellent opportunity for both of them to get back on track. So the king went back to his throne.

The first order of his agenda, Haghdar thought, was to see his best friend, the prince. He went to see him unannounced and came into his quarters. The prince was pleasantly surprised and smiled. Haghdar apologized for the time lost but told him about his conversation with the king and his promise to correct his ill behavior. He said he needed some time to get into shape and regretted to have wasted the valuable time of the prince all these years. He continued that it would not be long before he regained his strength and health both in body and mind. The prince told him he needed some exercise himself, and their time together would be for the utmost goal of bringing back the unification and glory to Faraaz nation and kingdom.

Next, Haghdar went to visit Raad, that is if it was still there. To his surprise, Raad had also lost weight, and some of its herd's youngest and strongest horses had lost hope and left. However, Raad's love for Haghdar was greater than its love for the other horses. Haghdar scratched under its chin with his right hand. He cited that he recognized his mistakes and he was immeasurably sorry for them, but he promised that, if forgiven by Raad, he would never abandon it again under any circumstances. He pleaded for just one more chance; however, if Raad decided against it, he would understand and treasure their love for as long as he lived. Raad looked into his eyes and saw that pleading gaze. They looked into each other's eyes for what appeared to Haghdar to be the longest time. Finally, Raad licked his hand as a gesture of accepting his apology, but only once to let him know that was his last and final chance. Haghdar understood and dropped his head in acceptance of Raad's condition.

So Haghdar and the prince started an extremely condensed training. They worked as hard as possible without wasting any time. They worked all day and planned into the night. The king of kings regularly sent them intelligence reports and instructed them to prepare plans to bring security to the country, to enforce law and order, and to punish those who violated Faraaz laws—specifically to draw war plans against those kings who declared their independence, did not pay taxes, and raised arms against Faraaz.

After a short six months, the prince informed the king they were ready to go back to the court and appear in public. The king ordered the necessary arrangements to be made for the ceremonious arrival of the prince and Haghdar. He invited the top generals and those kings who still were loyal to him to the reception festivity.

On the day the prince and Haghdar returned to the court, all dignitaries lined up to see them and what was made of them. Their excitement was mounting when Haghdar entered the court along with the prince. The king stood up and walked toward them. Haghdar, now in his late thirties, had gained his strength and was as tall and as strong as ever. They walked together to the throne, and as usual, the king sat on the throne with the prince on his right and Haghdar on his left at equal level. The king announced his pleasure with the return of Haghdar and the prince home and that their bond was stronger than ever. He proclaimed that all those who pledged their allegiance to the motherland and declared their loyalty to the king would be forgiven; for those who would not, the punishment would be severe and unprecedented. It was time for the Faraaz nation to be unified again under the just and fair laws of the kingdom and to prosper and flourish like never before.

The king turned to Haghdar and looked him in the eye. Haghdar knelt before the king and declared, "First I must apologize for my long absence and pray to the king of kings for forgiveness. I humbly admit my mistakes and would willingly accept proper punishment as determined by his majesty. Nevertheless, I wish to make a promise to the king of kings with my life; those mistakes will never happen again, and from now on, my entire life, whatever is left of it, will be devoted to serve my king and my country. Form this moment, I prefer to die a thousand times in the battlefield fighting for my favorite king and country than to live in indignity. My life belongs to my king and my country." The king nodded affirmatively and then stood up, took Haghdar's hand, and directed him to sit next to him on his left.

The king then turned to the prince and looked him in the eye as well. The prince knelt before the king and exclaimed, "My king, my hero, the king of kings, the greatest king ever was and ever will be, I must submit my most sincere apologies for my neglectful behavior, to have allotted my preferential agenda ahead of that of my country even though I believed they were intertwined. I am willing to accept, without question, any punishment his majesty finds suitable. However, if I live by the graciousness of my king's will, I will be a servant of my king and my country every second I live. I promise with my life that I will not allow anything or anyone to interfere in my path to truthfully serving my king and my country." The king nodded affirmatively, stood up, took the prince's hand, and directed him to sit next to him on the right.

The king then stated, "As previously noted, all those who submit their sincere regrets for their mistakes and pledge their allegiance to their king and to the Faraaz nation would be forgiven."

The audience saw the glare of happiness and confidence in the faces of the king, the prince, and Haghdar and bowed to the king. The king then declared it was time to attend to the affairs of the country without further delay.

The dignitaries present lined up according to their ranks and one by one apologized and pledged their allegiance to the king and to the Faraaz nation.

The king commanded his messengers to go to all corners of the kingdom and deliver his message to the other kings subject of the Fars kingdom. Many pledged their loyalty to the king of kings; a few were in disbelief and decided to go against the king's command.

The king, the prince, and Haghdar held regular meetings to plan war strategies against those kings who chose not to join Faraaz and remain disobliged. Haghdar and the prince regularly participated in the army maneuvers to practice but also to measure the new army's abilities. Many of the old generals and top warriors had retired; some had died. But overall, they were satisfied with the advances the army was making. They had to move fast. Time was of the essence.

HAGHDAR

Haghdar was determined to only think about saving his country and nothing else. At times he would subconsciously think about Shahrara and the good yet short time they had together but immediately diverted his thoughts to his conversation with and the promise he made to the king. He realized that by living in the past, he would lose the future—not only his own future and legacy but that of the king, the prince, and above all, his beloved country.

One afternoon, after a day's hard work, Haghdar and the prince were walking in the courtyard and talking about the final stages of their plans to punish disobeying kings when the prince casually asked if Haghdar had rid himself of his sadness completely. Once the wars started, there was no turning back and no room for any sensation other than victory. Haghdar said he thought of his wife and son from time to time, but unfortunately, there was nothing he could do about it at this time. Furthermore, he had rediscovered his greatest love, the love of his country. One must realize there is nothing that the passing of time would not heal. The prince jumped on his back, and they wrestled the rest of the way back to the palace, just like when they were eighteen years old.

CHAPTER TWENTY-FOUR

CALM BEFORE THE STORM

Haghdar and the prince took helm of the army in fights against the disobliged kings. Some of the kings, once seeing Haghdar and the prince leading the Fars troops, conceded immediately and prayed for pardon. They were arrested yet treated with respect and escorted to the court for prosecution and possible pardon by the king of kings since he was the only person with authority to grant clemency to the kings. Haghdar and the prince then announced that the warriors of those kings who conceded might put down their weapons. They would be pardoned upon pledging their allegiance to the king of kings. The high-ranking generals would be investigated and sent to the court for prosecution by judges, and respective rulings would be forwarded to higher court for the final decision.

Haghdar walked through files of warriors and talked to them to better understand their motives. Some of them had fought along Haghdar shoulder to shoulder against enemies in the past and expressed regret for their action. Haghdar was generous with them and condoned them.

One of the kings in charge of some territories in Toufan contacted the high council ruling Toufan in the absence of Haghdar and sought their guidance. He inquired about the council's position since the Fars army headed by the prince and Haghdar was speedily defeating other kings. They were getting closer to his region.

The high council advised him to concede before the Fars army even got close to his region and proceed to receive and greet Haghdar and the prince well before they got any closer. They said no man could defeat Haghdar in the battlefield, and they must retreat to other remedies. They advised him to greet Haghdar and the prince and their auspicious return to Toufan, where their gratifying leadership was critically needed. Toufan was slipping into trouble and needed their strength and wisdom to regain its position as an important part of the Faraaz nation.

On their way to Toufan, Haghdar and the prince received welcome messages from the aforementioned ruler and that he personally was arriving to submit his respect and apology as there seemed to be a misunderstanding on his part about the king of kings' instructions. Haghdar and the prince continued their campaign wary of the message. The ruler sent valuable gifts, the territory's most beautiful women—as there were many women who desired to wed either Haghdar or the prince—and the strongest horses to welcome their gracious arrival. Subsequent to his envoy, he arrived and was received by the prince and Haghdar in their jointly occupied quarters, where they were waiting for him to explain his misunderstanding.

The ruler stated that he had received the king of kings' commandment signifying those who had been unfaithful and committed treason would be pardoned upon submitting their sincere regret and pledging their allegiance to the king of kings. Notwithstanding the aforementioned mandate, he had never deviated from his pledge to the king of kings and therefore did not realize he must have pledged his loyalty again regardless of his obedience and faithfulness. This misunderstanding on his part was severe and deserved punishment, and he was there to submit himself for their decision. He added that his life belonged to the Fars kingdom, and in fact, it would be an honor to give his life for his great country and the king of kings. He continued, however, that his army had no knowledge of his misunderstanding and were on the assumption that his loyalty to the king of kings was established, evidenced by personally attending many wars against Fars enemies and that there was no delay in the payment of taxes to that date.

Haghdar stated they were content with the pledge of the ruler and admitted that misunderstandings might occur especially at times of turmoil. The prince added it was most appropriate that the ruler personally appear before the king and explain his misunderstanding. This would be an opportunity for him to meet the royalties, top generals, and court ministers. After all, it had been some time since he appeared before them. The ruler thanked the prince and Haghdar for their wisdom and graciousness and pledged he would send messengers to the court immediately to request permission to appear before the king of kings. The prince said that was not necessary as they already informed the king he was on his way. He trusted the ruler should not waste any time and must go immediately. The ruler expressed his gratitude and left without further delay.

After he left, the prince and Haghdar looked at each other and said, "What was that all about?"

They sent a message to the king to explain their meeting with the ruler and that he was on his way to the court. Haghdar and the prince sensed the ruler was not completely sincere, and there might be a bigger plot by the high council ruling Toufan, and they therefore decided to employ extreme caution. They knew there was no room for mistakes. They could not take any chance. The high council had ruled Toufan for more than a decade and had become very powerful; they were respected by the majority of Toufan's high-ranking generals, ministers, and priests and could cause major problems. They preferred to take over Toufan in peace and for Haghdar to become king again without war even though Haghdar had promised himself to never go back to Toufan after the passing of Shahrara.

CHAPTER TWENTY-FIVE

SURVIVING CATASTROPHE

Subsequent to the death of Shahrara, the high council of Toufan immediately accused the queen's chef of poisoning Shahrara because she discovered he was stealing and was to punish him. They confiscated the gold and other prizes they had given him as proof, convicted him of theft and murder, and executed him. They made allegations that the chef was able to steal from the queen with the help of Shahrara's most trusted servant, who had been a refugee since her death. She was wanted by the law, but her whereabouts had not been discovered. There were some rumors she was killed at the hands of some of Toufan's ship crew shortly after her escape.

After Fars defeated the king of Toufan and enclosed his country to the Fars kingdom, most family members of the king of Toufan were executed to prevent any attempt of coup d'état or uprising. However, one of Shahrara's nieces, five years old at the time, escaped and, some years later, went to the temple of the god of light as her sanctuary and became one of the servants there, living under a fictitious name. She grew to resemble Shahrara in appearance and character. She, at this time a teenager, had the same moonlight-pale skin, gold hair, and blue eyes. She did not talk much and found peace and safety only in serving the god of light. She heard about return of Haghdar and the Fars army and became fearful for her life since, in case her true identity was detected, she could be executed.

Toufan's high council had knowledge of her existence and true identity but did not take any action since she never left the temple. Additionally, arresting her on the temple grounds could deteriorate their reputation. There was no harm in allowing her to live and serve the god of light. They considered she was the only survivor descending from the king of Toufan and someday could be useful for their misfeasance purposes.

Toufan's high council received information that the said ruler was prompted to depart in order to appear before the king of Fars, and that could mean severe punishment for him and even execution. They realized the same fate might await them, especially if their scheme to kill Shahrara and her son was revealed. Haghdar and the prince were extremely intelligent, and the slightest mistake or discrepancy in their statements or any indication of sinister behavior or even thought would alarm them. Under those circumstances, and considering Haghdar's love for Shahrara, he could order the reopening of the case to commence a new investigation, which very well could end with their demise. In fact, Haghdar might have returned mainly to uncover the true cause of the queen's death. If that was true, he would not rest until and unless he solved the mystery of Shahrara and her son's death. They shivered with such thoughts as they knew that upon proof of their guilt, their death would be long and shameful with extreme pain. Moreover, their family members and relatives would be executed in front of their eyes first for the grand crime they committed. In their melancholy and sinful scheme of thoughts, they concluded the entire population of Toufan might be in jeopardy. Haghdar would be outraged once he found out how Shahrara and her son were killed and thereupon would not have mercy on anybody. They concluded that probably was what the king of Fars had in mind to begin with. The total destruction of Toufan as it was becoming too much of a problem. There were not many natural resources in Toufan, and the king had spent a large sum of wealth to rebuild it. They did not pay much taxes during the last several years and discontinued their communication with the king of Fars. They realized they were in a dire situation and needed a remedy, an increasingly dark scheme to cover up their crimes.

The high council concluded their only chance was to figure out Haghdar's weakness, no matter how insignificant it might be, in order to distract him from investigating his wife's death, and they even might get lucky and eliminate him for good. They reckoned their punishments would be beyond what any man could bear and therefore set themselves up for infinite shame, albeit they needed to plot a grave scheme to save themselves, their families, and relatives and, in the grand scheme of their crime, the people of Toufan.

The high council held long meetings and looked into all matters yet could not find a resolution to their dilemma. Haghdar was wise and could not be fooled easily, especially with the prince by his side. They did not dare to plot his assassination. Not even a hundred men could kill him; besides, his army was present and ready for war. The high priest members of the council suggested to visit the temple of the god of light to seek help from the old book. One of the generals suddenly recalled Shahrara's niece serving in the temple of the god of light. He cheerfully stated he might have a clue to remove the hindrance on the issue of Haghdar.

The high council decided to take the burden of a trip to the temple seemingly to praise the god of light for the return of Haghdar. They left the same night and rode without stopping to reach the temple as soon as possible. They came to the temple, and the high priest went directly to the hall where the arched skylight and old book of the god of light was placed. He saw Shahrara's niece sitting in the middle of the marble platform, meditating. The high priest stepped forward and called on her. She slowly stood up and gazed into the eyes of the high priest and saw the ominous look on his face. The priest calmly said, "Come, my child. There is a matter of utmost significance before us to discuss."

They entered a private room where the rest of the high council expected them. The top general opened the conversation and said they knew about her true identity for some time but did not wish to interfere with her services to the god of light. Even the enemies' services in the holy temple were not to be deterred. Alas, Haghdar was returning to Toufan, and he might not be as generous and forgiving as the high council. She must know Haghdar did not have mercy on Toufanians, their king, and even Shahrara. He killed all of them, committed the tradition to Shahrara and left her alone, and never looked back—not even after his wife and son were killed by the hands of a convicted cook. If he cared slightly for them by all accounts, he would at least come back to punish the cook himself as was customary. She knew this was a prelude to a more sinister scheme but, fearful for her life, bowed before the high council and, with a trembling voice, asked if she could be of service, to the high council's perplexity. The top general smiled in satisfaction and said that as a matter of fact, she could. The general continued that the only known family member of the king of Toufan who was not killed by Haghdar was Shahrara. Even though he committed the tradition and left her, he neither took her as a slave nor killed her as customarily was done. Therefore, he must have had some feelings for her. It had come to the attention of the high council that she increasingly resembled Shahrara and, like her, served the god of light. She must follow Shahrara's tactics to attract Haghdar's attention and emotions. In other words, she had the commission to make Haghdar to madly fall in love with her. The general continued that she most likely would be killed at the hands of Haghdar. Undoubtedly, he would come to the temple to pay his respects to the god of light and thereby would recognize her resemblance to Shahrara. However, if she did exactly as the council commanded, she might have a chance to live. Moreover, upon the completion of her mission, she might stay in the temple and live in peace for the rest of her natural life. Alas, if she was killed, it would be for her country, which she loved so much. Many Toufanian women gave their lives for their country, and in fact, it was an honor to die serving her country. The general asked if that was true. She dropped her head and passionately said that was true.

The general said, "Then it is settled." She said she was obliged by the council's conscientiousness for her beloved homeland. The high priest indicated that there was no time to spare, and they must proceed without further delay. They had to return to the court to greet Haghdar's arrival; meanwhile, she must appear and behave exactly like Shahrara. They would send Shahrara's makeup specialists and tailors to dress her properly. They would also contact her shortly with further instructions. The top general declared, as the last warning, that she must be aware that failure was not an option. She must succeed as, otherwise, many if not all, including herself, would perish by the hands of Haghdar, Toufan's sworn enemy.

The high council rode back to the court the same night and engaged in the preparations for the arrival of the prince, Haghdar, and the Fars army. Meanwhile, they assembled Shahrara's servants and staff and sent them to the temple of the god of light with instructions that Shahrara's niece must look and act exactly like her. They conveyed to them that Haghdar and the Fars army were coming to finish Toufan once and for all, and only she might save all. Accordingly, they must put their best effort to please Haghdar and, through Shahrara's image, deter him from his menacing intentions. The high priests sent a message to the priests in the temple, instructing them to create the setup and ambiance exactly similar to the time Haghdar met Shahrara.

The high council then went to greet and receive the prince and Haghdar a few kilometers out of the city. They had brought the best of what Toufan could offer, whether it be gold, jewels, or horses. Upon meeting the prince and Haghdar, they bowed before them and extended extreme pleasantries. They exclaimed that the reception of the prince and the great Haghdar returning to Toufan was the highest honor they could embrace, only second to receiving the king of the kings himself. They rode to the court, and the prince and Haghdar went to their quarters to freshen up and rest. That night they attended an expansive ceremony that the high council had arranged for them. The high council presented reports of the affairs of Toufan and prayed to the prince and Haghdar to wisely advise them for their shortcomings, of which they were certain. They declared Toufan fell into despair after the great Haghdar left. Indeed, they needed Their Majesties' instructions for any wrongdoing that might have taken place. The prince and Haghdar looked at each other; it seemed things were in order. Hence, they instructed the king's auditors to review reports and present their recommendations to the high council. The prince and Haghdar felt comfortable and thereafter relaxed. The prince said they had been riding for some time and would like some entertaining festivities, which immediately began. It was a calm and amusing night, and they enjoyed their time.

The next morning, the prince and Haghdar presided over the throne in reception of the ministers and dignitaries. They all greeted them and presented their gifts and expressed their utmost pleasure for the return of the prince and Haghdar. The top generals members of the high council reported military developments and requested the prince and Haghdar to attend the army maneuvers as it would immensely increase the personnel's morale, confidence, and abilities. The ministers requested permission for the general reception of Toufan's people. Such a reception, they said, would prove to the Toufanians once more that they were an integral part of the Faraaz nation. The prince and Haghdar patiently granted requests by the top generals and ministers and every night sent a message to the king, reporting the progress of the affairs. The high priests members of the high council were awaiting the proper opportunity to invite Haghdar to the temple of the god of light but did not want to rush it. They thought it was best that all Toufan's affairs were attended by the prince and Haghdar first so that when they invited them to the temple of the god of light, they were relaxed and satisfied with the high council's governance, ensuing their trust. They also thought Shahrara's niece needed some time to prepare for the main event.

One day, as the prince and Haghdar were in the reception of the high council, one of the high priests said it must be agonizing for the great Haghdar not having his queen by his side. The high council was extremely anguished, he claimed, for such a dreadful and deplorable event. Notwithstanding the somber occurrence, it was the tradition of the Faraaz nation for the king to visit the temple of the god of light upon returning to the throne to reflect devotion to our land and the god of gods, the god of light. The people of Toufan had a strong belief that such a visit would prove the praise of the god of light by their king. As such, they prayed to the prince and great Haghdar to concur with the Toufanians' belief. Haghdar felt his heart drop and took a pause for few seconds, which appeared to him like a lifetime. All eyes were on him; he looked at the high priest in the eye and said it was his intention to visit the temple just as soon as he finished his work in the capital. Nevertheless, even though he still was not done with his work, this would be a joyous visit. He could finish his work after his return. He therefrom instructed the high priests to make the necessary arrangements for their visit. The high priests bowed before the prince and Haghdar and stated it was Their Majesties' graciousness for which they were exceedingly grateful. The high priests requested permission for dismissal in order to attend to the affairs in preparation of the royal voyage, which was granted.

The high priests left supposedly to make necessary arrangements for the visit to the temple of the god of light by the prince and Haghdar. The high priests immediately sent messengers instructing priests and servants of the temple to make all the preparations. It was time that Shahrara's niece and Haghdar met. They emphasized that Shahrara's niece must look and behave exactly similar to Shahrara at the time she met Haghdar. No mistake was acceptable.

They also sent a message to Shahrara's niece, reemphasizing that her failure was not an option, and she would pay the highest price in case matters did not go exactly as they instructed. The high priest stated that further instructions would follow within a few days, during which time she must make Haghdar fall in love with her at all costs.

Shahrara's niece had been coached by the priests and servants of the temple who had witnessed Haghdar and Shahrara's first meeting and their time together. She was dressed and looked exactly like Shahrara to the point that no differences existed in appearance or character. They emphasized teaching her to talk like Shahrara, an attribute the priests had some difficulty to convey, but eventually she learned. It was more than a decade since Haghdar had left, and small differences under the circumstances, they thought, would go unnoticed by him.

The next day, the high priests requested permission to report the arrangements made for the prince and Haghdar's visit of the temple of the god of light and their guidance for any deficiency to the plans. The prince and Haghdar found the arrangements satisfactory and directed the high priests to carry on with the journey. The high priests requested permission to proceed with the departure of the prince and Haghdar the very next day, which was granted.

That night the prince and Haghdar held a meeting and discussed the high priests' motives for their move. They knew it was important to the beliefs of Toufanians and similarly the Fars nation to visit the temple of the god of light. It was important to them too since they believed in and worshipped the god of light themselves. But the high priests appeared too eager. They felt something was not right, especially, leaving the army in Toufan's capital and traveling with a handful of guards did not sound like a wise step to them. Mobilizing the entire army to the temple and therefore leaving the capital was an even worse idea.

They considered possible plots, including coup d'état by the high council. They therefore concluded it would be best that the prince stay in the capital, in charge of the army just in case there was a plot, and Haghdar visit the temple on behalf of both of them. The prince, during the meeting, casually cited that Haghdar did not have to take the trip if he did not want to. They could simply say there was an urgent matter that came to their attention the night before and postpone the visit. Haghdar smiled and replied that there was nothing to worry about. Besides, his visit to the temple would put all rumors to rest. Then he jokingly added that he was in control, but was the prince certain he could handle Toufan all by himself? They laughed at the anecdote and decided to call it a night.

Early the next day, Haghdar led the convoy to the temple. He told high priests some matter of urgency came up the night before, and therefore, the prince would not be able to accompany them at that time; he would visit the temple of the god of light at some other appropriate time. The high priests expressed their grief over such matters and requested permission for the movement of the envoy, which was granted.

The high priests could not be happier because the prince might have interfered with their plans and prevented them to follow through. They presumed the prince's absence was good luck, and the gods favored them in this life-or-death conspiracy. They sent messengers to inform all in the temple of their exact time of arrival, when

Haghdar would encounter scenes that were a replica of his first visit to the temple of the god of light.

Upon their arrival at the temple grounds, the high priests indicated that the great Haghdar might wish to be in the presence of the old book of the god of light in solitude to pray. Haghdar, not knowing about the high council's menacing plot, agreed. He told Raad not to worry because everything was under control and asked it to stay outside. He entered the temple and directly went to the hall where the old book of the god of light was placed. As he entered the hall, he saw Shahrara's niece. It was unbelievable; for a second, he thought she was Shahrara. She was dressed and disposed exactly like Shahrara, sitting in the middle of the marble platform with sunlight bouncing off the deck, portraying a rainbow on her face. She was calm and meditating, serving the god of light. Haghdar stood there in disbelief, thinking that all these years they lied to him. Why? As he came closer, he realized Shahrara should be in her late thirties by now while this girl was in her late teens. Still, she was a young Shahrara, as if she did not age one day since he saw her last. He came closer and asked her to stand up, which she did. He asked who she was. She said a servant of the temple of the god of light. She continued that she had heard about Great Haghdar and his visit to the temple; however, in the course of her meditation, she was dissolved in the greatness of the god of light and neglected the time and place. She proclaimed the god of light existed everywhere at all times; alas, not everyone was able to sense it. She stepped down from the platform and said Haghdar must be hungry and tired. They walked together into the dining area, where she prepared food and served to Haghdar. Haghdar asked her to sit down and accompany him. She sat and they ate together.

Then Haghdar mentioned he had been riding for some time and needed to rest. She took him to the same room Shahrara left him. The exact bowl of water and towels that smelled like fresh roses were already arranged. Haghdar washed up and lay down on the bed. He did not know what was happening to him. Was he joining Shahrara after all? He certainly deserved to be happy, even if it was for a little while. She could not, in all aspects, resemble Shahrara more yet was visibly receptive of him. She was not afraid to befriend him. She could make him happy, maybe happier than Shahrara because she was never married to the king of Toufan. For the first time since he left Shahrara to see his father before his passing, he felt the same sensations. He wanted to just be with her. He felt joy, to be young again, in the arms of young Shahrara. This time he would never leave her, always together. He would stay in Toufan as their king and serve the king of kings by prospering Toufan. He would raise their children and see them grow and become young and strong princes. He always wished to have a son to succeed him. He would teach him everything he knew, just like Zesht did for him.

In the midst of the contradicting waves of thoughts, they appeared all too crazy; what was he thinking? This could not be true. Was everything really under control? How could everything be exactly similar to the time he met Shahrara? The seeds of suspicion were planted in his mind and soul. Yet he had all kinds of emotions and could not differentiate truth from fiction. For the first time in a long while, he was not able to see the truth. Then he remembered the advice of his father, Zesht. They were playing chess, and Haghdar did not know his next move; Zesht told him, when in doubt, revert to your basics. Always trust your deepest feelings, and do not be afraid of them. They would guide you to the truth even though they might be painful and appear faulty.

Suddenly he recalled his promise to himself, his king, and the prince—the promise to spend the rest of his life to serve the kingdom and achieve the humane ideals the king and he developed and nourished for so many years. So much sacrifice was made for his country, the greatest love above all. So many lives were wasted. He was tired, so he tried not to reason with himself any longer and fell sleep shortly after.

The next day, Shahrara's niece woke him up and brought him breakfast. She always had a smile on her face and was ready to serve his every wish. She asked if she could make a request. Haghdar said, "Of course, what is it?" She said she would like to ride Raad, which was surprising to Haghdar. No person, not even Shahrara, would even think about riding Raad. It was too big and too proud to be ridden by anybody except Haghdar. He asked if she was sure; she said yes, that it was an honor to ride Raad. Haghdar said, "Let me talk to Raad and soften it up a little." Haghdar came to Raad and said Shahrara's niece requested to possibly ride the great Raad. It shook its head as a negative. Haghdar said, "Look, she is young, and this would be only a joy ride. It is actually good for you to feel a woman in the saddle. She is light, and it would not even feel like she is there." Haghdar said, "But be gentle with her and take it easy." Raad gazed at his eyes and recognized that pleading look, so it reluctantly licked his hand once, meaning that was the only time Raad would allow anybody other than Haghdar to have a ride. Haghdar said it was a deal.

That was a good day; she rode Raad and then they rode together, picnicked outside, and played hide-and-seek. Haghdar was very happy and laughed heartily. He played all day like a boy. It was some time since he had laughed and played last. He knew the temple servants were watching them from far but did not care. He was only having good time. That was all.

The servants at the temple were secretively watching Haghdar and her from far and regularly reported to the high priests about the occasions. The high priest's camp was in the temple's outbuilding, seemingly to allow Haghdar to meditate and pray in solitude. Judging by the rapid progression of events, the high priests concluded that Haghdar was madly in love with Shahrara's niece, and it was time to enter the next phase of their plan. Timing was of the essence and could not be spared. They were pleased to be ahead of schedule.

The high priests sent a message to Shahrara's niece, indicating it was time for her to finish Haghdar. They equipped her with the same dagger Shahrara used when she tried to kill him. They instructed her to go to his bedroom in the middle of the night and stand above his head and stab him in the heart with the dagger by both hands using all her strength. They emphasized Haghdar would not defend himself and would allow her to finish the job. Their plan was to immediately execute her upon the death of Haghdar, presumably in retaliation for the dreadful and unforgivable murder she committed. They would then declare she killed Haghdar to avenge the killing of her family and the invasion of her country.

CHAPTER TWENTY-SIX

ACTION

Shahrara's niece was fearful and reluctant to commit murder, which she knew she was not physically and mentally capable of. Many warriors tried to kill Haghdar in wars, only to be killed by him. Many assassination attempts to kill him had failed too. He had suffered injuries in wars that would certainly kill the strongest warriors yet survived. These injuries and afflictions made him stronger every time. He just seemed invincible; many kings would bow to his power and strength. Even the king of Fars, who had many warriors in his vast military each worthy of a kingdom, had said that without Haghdar, his empire would not be as strong. Considering his strength and survival instincts, she did not see how she would be able to kill him even if she stabbed him in the heart with the dagger. Her situation would be a lot worse in case she killed him one in a million chances. Therefrom, the news of Haghdar being killed by a woman from Toufan would travel fast. Many warriors would race from the four corners of the world to kill the person who killed Haghdar. She would be chased and tracked by practically every warrior, whether from the Fars military, other countries, or even small-time thieves and bandits, all kinds of madmen encouraged to kill the woman who killed Haghdar in order to make a name for themselves. She thought of why she had to suffer her entire life since the day she remembered. Her family members were massacred by the man sleeping sound in the next room as if nothing had happened. Nonetheless, she tried to live in secrecy, only to serve her god with no ego and no ambition, only dissolve in the goodness of her god, but now she was forced to make a choice, which could end with her demise regardless of the outcome. To her best estimate, she would live a few more days, if lucky.

Even so, she did not want to cowardly sneak upon Haghdar in the middle of the night and kill him on the temple grounds. She wanted to devote her entire life to the god of light and serve the best she could, but the occasion was grave. The whole situation was adversary and contradictory to the teachings of the old book of the god of light. She believed her soul would never be accepted by the god of light if she even thought of murder on the temple grounds. In fact, her soul would not have any place to settle in peace, neither this nor the next world, except in the darkness—the place for rejected souls by the god of light, where the gods of darkness ruled and grew. The thought of falling into the jurisdiction of the gods of darkness gave her a shiver. She felt a drop of cold sweat on her forehead, an indication of the presence of the agents of the gods of darkness in her inner self.

On the other hand, she thought, Haghdar killed all her family members, took over her beloved country, and forced her to live in disguise since the age of five. She decided if she was to be murdered, it was better for it to be a way of serving her country. She believed her soul would never be at peace, alive or dead, but not many choices were available. She reckoned there was no way she would live much longer either way. Nevertheless, the high council had made a promise to allow her to stay in the temple and serve the god of light if she was able to kill Haghdar. She might then request protection from the high council and, with some luck, change her identity so nobody knew who she was, just like the last fifteen years except with a different name, a different identity. She thought that was crazy enough to possibly work.

Hence, she waited until two hours past mid-night. She walked to Haghdar's bedroom lighter than spring breeze. Haghdar was sleeping and coincidently left the door half-open. Her heart was pounding; she was extremely excited. She could hardly breathe and almost sighed to take a deep breath. She peeked through the open door and saw Haghdar in a sound sleep. She quietly walked into the room, stood above Haghdar's head as instructed by high council, holding the dagger with both hands above her head, closed her eyes, and brought down the dagger with all her strength.

But a split second before the dagger ripped through Haghdar's heart, he opened his eyes and quickly grabbed her wrist close enough to his heart, where the tip of the dagger slightly cut his chest. She opened her eyes, observing the situation, which meant certain death sooner than she expected; she lost all control, forgot to breathe, passed out of fear and excitement, and fell on the floor. Haghdar immediately jumped out of bed, lifted her, and put her on the bed. He sprayed some water on her face and rubbed her shoulders to gradually bring her back to consciousness. She opened her eyes, not remembering what had happened for a few seconds. She saw Haghdar was standing by the bed and thought she was imagining things. She screamed, "God, what have I done? Please forgive me for disgracing the holy temple," when Haghdar took her hand and told her nothing had happened. She asked if they were alive, to which Haghdar answered affirmatively.

She started crying hysterically, begging for forgiveness as her actions were forced onto her against her will. Haghdar told her to be quiet and explain to him what she meant. She mumbled it was time for her to meet her demise, and her only wish was to be killed fast. Haghdar said nobody was to hurt her, and he understood she was under pressure. All he wanted to know was the truth. He said if she committed to the murder attempt under her own consciousness, the punishment would be execution; notwithstanding, he believed she must have been forced to commit such a horrific crime, and therefore, she would be pardoned if she disclosed the truth to him. She asked Haghdar to give his word as he never turned his back on his word. He said, "Haghdar gives you his word." She started to describe all that had happened, that she was Shahrara's niece living incognito since the elimination of her entire family some fifteen years ago. She continued, all she wanted was to serve the god of light, but the high council knew about her identity, her resemblance to Shahrara, and Haghdar's love for Shahrara. The high council's scheme was to make him fall in love with her and then to kill him, just like Shahrara attempted to kill him. They emphasized Haghdar would not defend himself even if he woke up. She stated her choices were either to refuse the high council's offer, in which case they would kill her as a member of Toufan's royalty, or to kill Haghdar. The high council had promised her immunity and that she could live in the temple and serve the god of light for the rest of her natural life. Haghdar told her they were both in serious danger and must go back to the prince secretly in the middle of the night. The prince might be in danger too, only if it was not too late already.

They immediately left the temple and went to Raad. Haghdar put his finger on his lips to show Raad they must be quiet. He saddled Raad and told it must run faster than the wind. In case high priest and their guards caught up with them, they would try to kill all three of them. Raad understood and nodded affirmatively.

CHAPTER TWENTY-SEVEN

ARRESTED

Haghdar and Shahrara's niece arrived at Toufan's palace in the middle of the next night. They went directly to the prince's quarters and, despite the guards' protests, walked into his bedroom. The prince woke up and saw Haghdar with Shahrara. He could not believe his eyes and, for a second, thought Shahrara was alive. The prince was exceedingly happy and praised the god of light for keeping her alive. Haghdar lit some light and told the prince that a matter of extreme urgency was before them. Haghdar introduced Shahrara's niece and explained the high council's scheme to assassinate him and possibly the prince afterward. The prince inquired about the high priests' whereabouts since supposedly they traveled with Haghdar to the temple of the god of light. Haghdar said they were in the temple when he left but might have relocated since then. Haghdar asked about the rest of the members of the high council. The prince said they were in their quarters but must be prevented from escaping as news traveled fast. The prince immediately called on his top guards and warranted the arrest of the members of the high council. The prince's instructions were to arrest the members of the high council; they were to be brought before him alive.

Early morning after the night Shahrara's niece was supposed to kill Haghdar, the high priests came to the temple, assuming she finished the job. They went to Shahrara's niece's bedroom, but she was not there. They ran to Haghdar's bedroom, and he was not there either. They searched for Raad, but it had disappeared too. The high priests realized what must have happened and decided to run for their lives. They had to vanish if they wished to live to see the light of another day. And so they did not waste a second and left the temple with their most trusted guards, those willing to give their lives for the benefit of the priests. The priests decided to somehow find their way to Mantik and seek safety in the temple of Mantik's previous king, now rumored to be a sanctuary for bandits and wanted outlaws.

Back in the court, the rest of the high council members were arrested and brought before the prince and Haghdar. They were confronted with Shahrara's niece and given an opportunity to explain themselves. The remaining members of the high council, top generals, and ministers denied any knowledge about everything she said or did and that she must be punished severely for her crime. The law was clear about the punishment, which was a painful death, they reflected. They claimed further that if, in fact, the high priests had commissioned her to assassinate Haghdar, they must be punished as well. They claimed they were ashamed of themselves to have had any association with and in fact trusted them. The prince and Haghdar did not believe their statements and therefore declared that the high council members would remain in contempt until the completion of their investigation. The prince ordered the troops to go to the temple of the god of light, to arrest high priests, and to bring them to him for proper prosecution.

The prince also sent a message to the king of kings to inform him of the assassination plot and to seek advice from his father. The king of Fars sent a message back, requiring all arrested to be sent to Fars under the strictest security as there might exist a bigger plot in the works. The king's instructions was that the high council members must be separated from their operators at once; nothing could be left to chance. The king charged that the ruler of Toufan territories who previously came to Fars was also under arrest, and once confronted by the members of high council, the truth could be revealed. The king of kings advised the prince to tighten security in the entire Toufan, especially in the army's chain of command, where top generals might still have faithful subordinates, that the prince himself take over the army's command and Haghdar and Shahrara's niece to go back to Fars. They had firsthand information about the entire plot. Time was not to be spared. The prince must not trust anybody, with the exception of the most faithful members of Javidan. The army's chain of command must immediately be delegated to the top officers of Javidan until further notice from the king.

The investigative troops arrived at the temple of the god of light and found it empty. High priests and their guards, temple employees, and servants had deserted the temple and escaped or gone to hiding. The troops searched for their traces and were able to find and arrest a few of them hiding in the vicinity of the temple grounds. They were transported in chains back to the court without further delay. The captain of the troops selected some of the best guards and personally led them to find and arrest the high priests and their devoted guards.

The prince received another message from the king of kings to send those arrested on the temple grounds to his court for the trial of the century as no general of Fars had betrayed his king to the point of murder in recent memory. So they were chained and sent to Fars under strict security measures. Haghdar led the envoy, and the prince stayed in Toufan to prevent any revolt or uprising. The prince also conducted a comprehensive and profound investigation to identify any of the high council members' subordinates who may have carried or helped with the assassination plot.

CHAPTER TWENTY-EIGHT

THE PUNISHMENT

Haghdar came to Fars bringing high council members and servants of the temple of the god of light in chains and went directly to the court, where he was expected by the king. Haghdar entered the court, and as usual, the king stood up from the tribunal and walked to him to greet his arrival.

Haghdar bowed before the king and observed the customary courtesies. The king held his hand in his and invited him to sit next to him on the left-hand side of the throne. Haghdar requested permission to proceed with the hearing without delay, which was granted. The king ordered the ruler of Toufan territories whom previously was sent to Fars by the prince and Haghdar to be brought in for the hearing as well. The king then declared that the accused may one by one state their cases to be heard by the court ministers. The purpose of the hearing was to discover the truth. The accused must realize that any attempt to conceal or falsify facts would add to their charges and therefore more severe punishment. They must understand that the punishment could go beyond simple death; hence, only the truth might save their souls and dignity and that of their families and loved ones. The king declared that the final decision would be made upon receiving the verdict of the court ministers by the king and Haghdar solely based on the facts presented.

HAGHDAR

The captured members of the high council pleaded not guilty. They maintained their position that they had no knowledge of the high priests' plot and they were guilty to the extent they did not discover their mischiefs. They denied any involvement with or knowledge of plans to murder Haghdar and hence prayed to His Majesty to be punished for their negligence.

The servants of the temple of the god of light in Toufan confessed to have participated in the high council's treason, to the extent that they made necessary arrangements in order for the great Haghdar to fall in love with Shahrara's niece but had no knowledge of assassination plot. They only carried the orders and had no role in or knowledge of planning their treacherous crime. They also admitted they should have immediately informed the prince and Haghdar of such activities rather than carry on with the mission. They added the high council's instructions were vivid, either to report the progress of events in the temple or be executed. They pleaded guilty and prayed for the majesties' graciousness on their families.

The guards claimed they had no knowledge or any involvement in the assassination plans; they did not carry any order other than solely to protect the temple, the envoy led by Haghdar, the high priests, and the servants against any outside threat, which was their primary and only job. They declared the high council never showed them any indication about their assassination ploy. They knew the guards would immediately report it to their superiors. Further, the orders to accompany Haghdar and the high priests to the temple were given by the top generals who were their direct superiors, and they, in turn, received their orders from Haghdar himself. Moreover, they had always obeyed the commands of their superiors and never questioned or detested any of their commands or motives.

The ruler of Toufan territories also refuted any knowledge of the plot but admitted he received his orders from the high council directly. He admitted receiving and following the high council's orders for the reason they told him Haghdar would never come back to Toufan again, and they were appointed by the king of kings to govern Toufan as they saw fit. He assumed their superiority since the high council was appointed originally by Haghdar. He did not contact the king of kings or Haghdar because he never pulled a shortcut over the chain of command.

The king and Haghdar listened to all the statements made by the accused patiently. The king had received information in conformity with the statement of the ruler of the Toufan region to a certain degree. He also knew he preferred to serve the high council over the king and had ambitions of his own, especially with regard to not paying taxes. He was promised autonomy by the high council. The king inquired about the court council's verdict. The speaker of the council requested some time to go over the evidence and testimony presented. The king called the hearing adjourned until the next morning. The accused remained under contempt. The king asked Haghdar to go to his quarters to discuss certain matters.

Once in the king's quarters, he asked Haghdar's opinion. Haghdar said he did not believe the ruler's statement to be completely true; however, he did not feel like he was a part of the assassination plot. Haghdar continued that the high council did not think the ruler was intelligent enough to get him involved in the decision-making process. The king said that since Haghdar was gone, he had all kinds of excuses for the late payment of taxes, and then there were some inconsistencies in his statements with which Haghdar concurred. They decided he did not have the merits to be a ruler, but he did not deserve to be executed either. The king reflected on the guards. Both the king and Haghdar agreed that even though they had nothing to do with the high council's scheme, they were not capable of guarding royalties. The high council members obviously were guilty as accused; the temple servants confessed and testified to those facts. They deserved a disgraceful death. All their properties would be seized and their family members under house arrest for the rest of their lives. The king stated that the temple servants helped with the high council's plot; however, whether they had any knowledge of the assassination was unknown.

The king said no servant of the temple of the god of light was executed as far as the history showed. Accordingly, they would be discharged from the temple with disgrace and be imprisoned for the rest of their lives without the possibility of parole. Their family members may keep their properties and live as free citizens. The king stated they needed some rest and therefore called it a night.

The next day, the court council presented their verdict, which was the execution of all of them except for the guards who were to be discharged from the military.

The king of kings declared that after reviewing the council's verdict, there was no ambiguity about the law and the respective punishment for such an atrocious crime. The council recommended, except for the guards, execution for the accused. However, he would have mercy on those who acted without knowledge of the assassination or with negligence. Accordingly, the guards would be demoted and put on probation; the ruler of Toufan territories would be exiled with his family members. The servants of the temple would be discharged from serving the god of light. They would be imprisoned for the rest of their lives. Their family members would be entitled to their property without any visitation rights. The members of the council were convicted of the highest crime and therefore would be shamefully executed. Their names would vanish from the pages of history and must not be heard ever again. Their properties would be seized except for a limited amount allotted to their families. They must leave Faraaz and never come back. In case any of the high council's family members were to be seen anywhere in the entire Faraaz, they would be executed.

The high council dropped their heads in acceptance of their sentence. Deep in their hearts, they were grateful for their families to be spared. They did not say a word about murdering Shahrara because they knew that in case it was revealed, their family members would be sentenced to the same painful and prolonged death.

It was a somber time for all particularly Haghdar. These proceedings brought painful memories of the loss of Shahrara and the son he never saw. He would never know the truth about the death of Shahrara and his son. Haghdar was crying deep inside. The king sensed Haghdar's pain and joined him in spirit and cried deep inside too.

CHAPTER TWENTY-NINE

THE CLIMB

Zodiak left the temple in Mantik after dark. He moved as fast as he could to get to the foot of the mountain before anybody saw him. He was not superstitious and did not believe Ahreman lived at the bottom of the canyon. There could be some kind of large python symbolic of Ahreman, some kind of beast, man-eating animal, or the likes of it; hence, he had to fight his way through. He knew it would not be easy; in fact, it was a very dangerous journey, but he intended to complete the mission. It was the mission of his life to accomplish in solitude and with the help of no one.

Zodiak remembered his mother's last words that someday he would be king. Those words were the only help he needed. The remembrance of his mother's words raised his courage and shone a ray of hope on his heart. He thought his mother was a servant of the god of light, a wise person who rarely was wrong. She must have known some truth nobody else could have perceived.

Throughout the first few weeks of his journey, Zodiak mostly rested during the day and traveled at night, just to make sure nobody saw him. He had to hunt at dawn or dusk in order to prepare food for the next day or two. He had to travel to higher grounds first to reach the top of the canyon and then down to the bottom of it. From there he needed to climb on the other side of the canyon to reach on top of the highest mountain, where Seepar was said to have lived. As he climbed higher and higher, there was plenty of water to drink and wash. He had long learned to be self-sufficient since his mother's death. After few weeks, he came atop the canyon between mainland and the foot of the mountain on the other side, a remote place with not many people around. The few people who lived there were secluded from the rest of the world since no-body traveled into or out of that godforsaken place; there was no news or information, a land of nomads. They simply paid no attention to Zodiak as he passed by. To them he was another lost soul wandering around in search of food or water, a life not much above those of animals.

Farther toward the top of the canyon, where he had to start his downhill trip, Zodiak noticed rotten animals' corpses and some remains of human bones. It was clearly an indication of certain death surpassing that of life. Zodiak passed over them, thinking there would be many dead upon whom he would have to walk if he wanted to achieve his goal—to conquer Fars and the world, to find those who killed his mother, and to find his father. He felt strength in his image beyond what any man could grasp. He thought this was the time to achieve his long pursued goal or else preferred not to live at all. He knew at this stage of his life and after all he had been through, he would not want to live if he could not achieve his ideals. He felt most determined, a feeling that made him physically and mentally strong—the kind of strength in solitude that could not be tarnished or shattered. He knew there were many agents of the gods of darkness on his path against whom he had to prevail.

Through all these fast-moving thoughts, he began to gradually think it was not power per se he most desired but the power to destroy and omit those evils that were the cornerstones of all mischief. He pondered that he must make the world a better place for all once he killed and then gained the powers of Seepar. Yet he knew his childhood memories had long conquered his heart and soul despite his strength and wisdom; he was never to be free.

The mountain on top of which Seepar was said to be living was either accessible from the south side of the mountain, where the king of Mantik once had approached, or the east, the route Zodiak had chosen. The east side of the mountain, if one could climb to the top, ended onto the back of the bedrock on top of which Seepar was assumed to be living. The east side right behind Seepar's nest was an extremely steep and deep cliff with some ninety-degree grade ending in a vast and deep canyon. Zodiak had to get to the bottom of the canyon, where myth said Ahreman lived, cross the canyon, and then start climbing on the other side to arrive at the back of the bedrock, presumably to surprise Seepar. Zodiak wondered which part of the journey could be more dangerous—climbing to the top or killing Seepar. But then again, these thoughts could deteriorate his resolve. He simply decided to only think of victory—achieving his goal. Zodiak found strength in his mind and soul; he reckoned if he could not get to the top of the bedrock, he did not deserve to rule the world anyway.

He therefore started sliding down toward the bottom of the canyon. From there he could begin climbing the ninety-degree cliff all the way to the top of the mountain covered by the clouds—easier said than done.

Each step, Zodiak knew, got him closer to his target and hence carried higher danger. His heart was pounding and tempered with every step—a journey worth taking if for no other reason.

Zodiak decided to travel during the day since there was nobody else in that vicinity and rest at night. He thought it would be safer for him to face any danger, whether going downhill or fighting beasts, during the day and camp at night, when he would hopefully be secure from any attack by wild animals as long as he stayed close to his campfire. He had to hunt during the day, if he had the chance, and prepare meals at night. The climate got drier and drier and dustier as he went lower and the hunting far and in between. He decided to ration his food and water since it could be days before he had any chance to hunt again or find water, that was if he got lucky. After several weeks of going downward, he had a vague glimpse of the bottom of the canyon.

As he slid lower, he noticed some small streams running between rocks and ending in a river at the bottom of the canyon. Amazingly, the river at the bottom of the canyon was not visible from above where he started sliding down-ward. Big boulders and twisted elevated grounds blocked the view of the river. In other words, he thought, water and food. It was a pleasant surprise. He was eager to get there before the dark since animals, if any, would come to drink late afternoon or early evening. Zodiak considered to have passed the first stage of his journey—maybe the easiest part yet the most important one. For obvious reasons, he would never be able to get to the top of the mountain if he did not get to the bottom of the canyon. He felt warmth in his heart, and hope glimmered in his spirit. Zodiak decided to camp there to gather food and water for at least the next few days since he did not know when he would fancy them again. Upon arriving at the river, he waited for his hunt despite his eagerness to wash up and play like a child given his favored toy. As he expected, shortly thereafter, some birds and mountain goats showed up to drink. Zodiak was happy, and the thought of good food and clear water washed away all his anxiety. As he was getting ready to make his hunt, a large alligator emerged from the water, and before he could make a move, it bit and swallowed a large goat. The rest of the animals ran away and the alligator submerged back to the bottom of the river.

The alligator was extremely large and powerful. Zodiak estimated it must have been some ten meters long and eight hundred to one thousand kilograms, almost one metric ton. Zodiak knew that as long as the alligator lived, not only he could not get food or water, but he also was obstructed from crossing the river in order to continue his journey. The beast was living between him and the other side of the river, where he must start his climb. He went back to his little campfire, thinking how he could get rid of the monster. The next day, early in the morning, he went back to the river, pretending to be drinking water yet awaiting the alligator to show up. He used himself as bait to drag out the monster. To no doubt, the beast showed up and, with mind-boggling speed, opened its jaws to swallow him. Zodiak, a master swimmer since childhood, dove into the water with lightning speed, swam under the alligator's belly, and pushed his sword into its heart with all his strength. The alligator started to roll over, and the river turned red with its blood. Zodiak swam deeper and came out on the other side of the river, waiting for the alligator to die. After more than two hours, the alligator stopped moving. Zodiak knew it was dead, went to the alligator, and claimed his sword. He waited for sunset to finally make a hunt before starting his climb the next morning.

After his hunt, he washed up and made a small fire, prepared his food, and consumed enough. It was the first time since he started his journey to fancy a full stomach and no worries for the night. He spent some time to make food for the next several days since he did not know when he would be able to make his next hunt. He was pleased and fell asleep fast in front of low-burning fire.

The next day, early in the morning, he woke up and ate a light breakfast, put out the campfire, and looked around to find best climbing path to the top. The cliff was too high, and clouds covered the top of the mountain. They did not allow him to see his path all the way to the top. He decided to select his way up in parts. Each part led to a small place, where he could camp for the night and take it from there. He started climbing rocks and pulled himself up one small step at a time. A couple of times, his hand slipped and he almost fell, but he was able to hang on and grab another rock. He learned early on to fix his feet and hands on stable rocks to avoid slipping and falling. After a few months of climbing, he came to a small place in the middle of the cliff and decided to camp for the night. He had to tie himself to a rock to make sure he did not fall off in case he tossed and turned in sleep. The next day, he woke up and chose his next path as far as it was visible. His climb continued many months when gradually food and water became the primary concern. Even with the tight ration he allowed himself, he had food and water only for a few days. Zodiak had to look for and hunt while climbing, which seemed impossible; not even mountain goats could reach there. He had some water. He also consumed water by absorbing the humidity running between the cold rocks, but food was scarce. Therefore, he decided to set a trap in case he saw a prey, which meant he had to use his remaining food to attract any living. This could be fatally dangerous in case he used his ration but was not able to hunt. He thought he had no other choice, not knowing what his fate had laid in front of him.

As he climbed higher, it was getting harder and harder to balance and find a grip. Sometimes he was hanging before he could find a footing. Under those circumstances, he suddenly saw an eagle flying in that vicinity. The eagle saw him too, and in one moment, both in the air, one flying and the other hanging, their eyes met. They both knew one of them would be dinner. As the eagle flew closer, Zodiak realized it was a very large one with a dead look in its eyes, which would make any ordinary man shiver. Zodiak fixed his feet; he knew this bird did not need a trap. He was the bait for it. Zodiak immediately fastened himself to a rock by the rope, holding his sword by his teeth. Suddenly, the eagle picked up speed and flew right toward him to break his neck with one strike of its large and strong talons in order to kill him on the spot. As soon as the eagle was within arm's length extended by the sword, he chopped the eagle's neck with one strike of his sword and grabbed it with another hand before it fell to the bottom of the canyon. He thought, with tight rationing, the hunt should provide sufficient food for next several days or maybe weeks. It was not exactly his favored meal, but he had to eat what he could get, no complaints.

Zodiak continued climbing the steep cliff. As he reached higher, the climb was more difficult, and therefore, he moved slower. The only hunt he could get was birds and not too many of them but enough to keep him alive. After almost two years since he started his journey, he was getting close to the top of the mountain, right under the bedrock.

CHAPTER THIRTY

THE WINNER

Zodiak reached the top of the mountain and very quietly climbed to the edge of the bedrock from behind. His plan was to run toward Seepar as soon as he reached on top of the bedrock and cut its legs to prevent it from running or flying away. He could then kill Seepar and wash himself in its blood. So he waited a few moments under the bedrock, took a deep breath, and with one acrobatic move, jumped over the bedrock, but Seepar was nowhere to be seen. He started to cautiously search for the big bird, but it was not there. He thought maybe the myth was not true. Maybe the priest lied to him about his encounter with Seepar because he assumed Zodiak would never reach the top of the mountain. The priest probably assumed he would die on his way and never come back. He would continue his lies without any evidence to the contrary. On the other hand, somehow he was able to receive pardon from the king of Fars. But how? Obviously, he could fool many people, especially the superstitious ones who had believed in Seepar for hundreds of years. Naturally, the priest was making his own legacy by representing himself as the only man who ever encountered with Seepar and lived to tell about it.

Zodiak then thought his plans were all ruined, his reputation a fool, and his words forever unbelievable. Nobody would believe he actually climbed to the top of bedrock on top of the highest mountain only to find there was no Seepar, that it was all a story. He was the only person to know the truth—albeit there was no way he could prove this. Without doubt, the priest would contradict him and continue his claim of fighting Seepar. He was the only man alive to tell about it. He lost hope and sat on a rock, thinking of what he should do now. People would mock him for being a nomad, crazy, a lost soul with no place to live, no place to go. Some might even say Seepar took his soul away and let him live as a dupe, a shell of a man. But the worst part was that he would never be able to defeat Fars. On top of that, he would never know his father. It seemed to be over for him.

As he was drowning in those gloomy thoughts, a deep and frightening voice from behind called, "I know you." Zodiak turned around and saw Seepar behind him. It was nothing he had ever seen or imagined before. Seepar was huge yet sleek, with a beak that was stronger than steel and sharper than his sword. With no emotion in its eyes and a dead look, Seepar was staring at him, a gaze which pierced through his heart and soul. Its claws were like giant iron hooks. They could tear apart any being with one strike. Its wings spread more than twenty meters on each side, with colors of the night, deep and dark purple, comingled with such a burned gray ebony and hardened clogged red blood, the kind of mixed dark colors that absorbs light in its abstraction. The myth did not do justice in describing its size, fearful appearance, and strength. For a moment, he thought if there was a way to get out of that mess alive.

Zodiak shook himself and remembered why he was there. Nothing could or should change anything now. He must think about one and only one thing—killing the enemy. Seepar saw resolve in Zodiak's eyes. It knew this young man.

Seepar said, with the same frightening voice, "I know you and I know why you came here, but there are some truths you need to know first." Zodiak replied that there was no truth he was seeking there, and if in fact, Seepar knew the reason for his journey, there was nothing else to discuss. Seepar expressed, "You must know in part you are of me and fighting me is essentially fighting yourself. The same goes for me. If I consume you, I have consumed a part of myself, and that is something neither of us should do. Lower your weapon, and I will reveal the truth to you. You will find answers to all your questions and ambiguities." Seepar continued, "Your life has been full of pain with a superb turn of events. Nonetheless, the truth will hurt you more. Hence, you must be able to understand certain rationalities before I could tell you the entire truth about your life, who you are, why certain people sought to kill you and your mother, and what lay ahead of you."

Those words penetrated Zodiak's heart and made blood rush to his head, remembering all his sufferings—never seeing his real mother, finding out about her murder, living in disguise most of his life, and never knowing who his father was. He felt pain, very dramatic pain apparently inflicted by Seepar. So he replied, "Enough talking. You said your piece. Now let us get down to business." Zodiak was not there for pleasantries and took a position to fight. Seepar said one last time, "You are making an irreversible mistake. Let me open your eyes to the truth." Zodiak shouted it was all right with him because all his life he had been wrong, and look where that got him now.

Seepar suddenly blew its breath toward Zodiak, a heavy and repulsive air-stream that made him dizzy and almost knocked him out. He immediately covered his mouth and nose with his scarf. Seepar opened its wings, which caused heavy wind to blow in his direction. Then Seepar took to the skies and came down with unimaginable speed to strike his neck with its claws. Zodiak dodged the blow by jumping behind a boulder and waited for Seepar to attack again. He took off all his clothes at once while hiding behind the boulder. Seepar took to the skies again and this time circled above his head and, in less than a second, came down and struck Zodiak's chest. The blood started running all over Zodiak's body.

The battle was ferocious, and both fought relentlessly. After hours of fighting, both were severely injured and tired. Zodiak thought he could not defeat Seepar without an effective and innovative plan. Therefrom, he must take advantage of one fortunate moment to put his sword into its heart, flying above his head, and then hold it on top of him with a tree trunk he took from Seepar's nest for as long as he could. He then could wash himself in its pouring bloodstream. Easier said than done, but he had no other choice.

His only hope was to fight Seepar off until the fortunate moment presented itself. Zodiak jumped between two rocks narrowly adjacent with his sword in his hand and the tree trunk on his side. He chose that place because it was not wide enough for Seepar to reach him. As Seepar flew down to grab him with its claws in order to pull him out of the hiding place, Zodiak put his sword into its heart with all his strength and simultaneously lifted the tree trunk and put it vertically under the Seepar. Seepar fell, and the tree trunk tore right into its body, and the stream of blood started to run. Zodiak had already rid himself of all his clothing and therefore opened himself to its bloodstream. Seepar's blood covered Zodiak's entire body, except he blinked for an epsilon of time, when the blood did not go into his left eye. Zodiak never noticed this incident and made sure blood covered everywhere else on his body, from the top of his head to the tip of his toes. He was injured and extremely tired. So before he could recognize the extent of the impact of the event on his life, he lost consciousness. On the other hand, before taking its final breath, Seepar saw Zodiak's fault, and a burning glow flashed in its eyes.

Zodiak did not know how long it was before he came to consciousness. He pulled himself out from between the rocks. He then gradually started to remember what had happened. First he looked at himself. To his surprise, his body was healed, and no trace of any injury existed. He was not tired either, and in fact, he felt fresh and strong. He looked around and found no trace of Seepar except some ashes. All of a sudden, a strong wind blew the ashes into the air. They vanished before Zodiak could get his hands on any part of them.

Zodiak noticed his strength was increasing, his wisdom maturing, and his spirit flying. He understood the changes. He was ready for the next step in his life, which was to conquer the world. He thought it was time for him to materialize all his dreams and make the world a better place for all where there were no lies, no cheating, and no killing. He had to clean up the world of those who did anything and everything for power and money and served the gods of darkness. Yes, it was time.

Zodiak decided to take the south side of the mountain to go back to Mantik because it was shorter and more convenient. He wanted to pay a visit to the priest, to explain to him his revised plans, which was not for the purpose of making him king. In fact, he thought, what would make the world need a king? Power and wealth. All this killing, deceit, and betrayal so one person could impose superiority over others for his selfish and malignant satisfaction, this must stop, and he was the man to do it. He intended to invite the priest to join forces with him to achieve his vision of a better world for all and to find his father. He felt he was ready and capable of understanding and accepting the truth about his mother, father, and himself.

CHAPTER THIRTY-ONE

SUCCESSION

The king of kings was old by then, and the priests and doctors had told him he did not have much time to live. He had made all the necessary arrangements for the Faraaz nation to continue to thrive for many years to come. He also had made sure for justice and equality to expand to the farthest points of the empire. Many justice posts had been established all around the country in order for the people to voice their complaints and requests. These justice posts were governed by the most trusted and devoted judges and prosecutors. Additionally, he sent special envoys to directly speak with citizens to inquire about the handling of their complaints and requests by the justices.

Consequently, except for minimal local disturbances by some outlaws and bandits, the entire empire was in peace, and economic and social programs were progressing according to his plans. The Faraaz nation was prospering in many different ways and levels. The fundamentals of a free, just, and equitable social system with increasing organic wealth and fortunes were all in place. The king knew that with proper governance, the Faraaz nation will continue to grow financially, socially, and in other areas for a long time into the future. However, the process of succession still was not settled to his satisfaction. Particularly, his main concern was the succession of the prince since the top generals, priests, and court ministers still reminded him from time to time to organize the council to be headed by the prince and Haghdar. Time was short, and although the grounds were not exactly as he had wished to resolve the issue at hand, the king made up his mind and called Haghdar and the prince to his chamber—albeit the king of kings had no doubt about Haghdar's loyalty, yet he needed to make sure Haghdar agreed to the prince's succession and the prince understood Haghdar would cogovern the Faraaz nation. He wanted each of them to understand that the empire might not prosper without either of them. The kingdom needed a king, a master politician and war strategist, and Haghdar, a master of leadership and execution.

Haghdar and the prince came to the king's chamber where, he was sitting on a chair comfortably. They both paid their respects and observed customary courtesies. The king asked them to sit with him since there was an issue of extreme importance to discuss. The king ordered some food and drinks to create the atmosphere of a home where decisions were made by the family rather than the head of the state.

The king started by saying he would not live much longer according to the doctors and priests. The prince and Haghdar dropped their heads somberly. The king continued, "Such is life. Death is the price for life." There would always be an end to life as long as there was a beginning, but what should not end was the prosperity of the empire and Faraaz nation. Their achievements, or that of the Faraaz nation, must not conclude with his death. To that end, he believed the continuation of the fortunes of the Faraaz nation would ultimately be dependent on the succession. Next king must extend existing programs and, at the same time, have his own vision for the growth and happiness of the entire Faraaz nation as the time changes—not an easy task. In fact, he believed his soul would not be accepted by the god of light if he was not able to warrant a proper succession. The king added that top generals, priests, and court ministers expressed their wishes to organize a council consisting of the most trusted of them handpicked by the king himself and headed by the prince and Haghdar to lead the Faraaz nation. Accordingly, most, if not all, authorities to make decisions presently bestowed upon the king would be delegated to the council with each member being entitled to one vote. The prince and Haghdar would have the right to veto the council's decision for three times; alas, in case the council approved of the same measure for the fourth time by unanimous vote, the prince and Haghdar would have to accept and comply with the decision. The council would never be entitled to vote the prince and Haghdar off the council nor remove them from office as the head of the council. The king declared the top generals, priests, and ministers were faithful servants of the Faraaz nation, whom he unconditionally trusted; however, he had decided for the prince and Haghdar to jointly take helm of the throne. He did not think that such a council would be as decisive and fast-paced as the two of them. This meant the prince and Haghdar must make vital commitments not to allow anything or any person to come ahead of what was in the way of the Faraaz nation's prosperity and progress. The two of them must unconditionally trust and rely on each other for as long as they lived. The king wanted them to make such a commitment and promise to never have secrets from one another. They must make all sacrifices for the Faraaz nation should it become necessary, even if it meant to give their own lives or that of their loved ones. From that moment, nothing and nobody could and neither should be more important than the goodness of the empire. The rest of their lives must be totally and completely devoted to serving the great nation of Faraaz. Let it be known for eternity of time that nothing could defeat them as long as they kept their promise and commitment to these humane and profound ideologies. That succession of the king of kings was prompted by the weighing of their qualifications, and nothing else was taken into consideration.

The prince and Haghdar looked at the king with tears in their eyes. They were speechless, for no words could surpass that of the king and his manifest. After a few seconds, Haghdar exclaimed his commitment. He said an important part of his soul would be lost with the passing of his favored king. His wisdom would never be replaced, and it was with a heavy heart that he admitted the facts of life. The prince declared his life had and would always be spent in the way of the teachings of the king of kings. He held Haghdar's hands, looked into his eyes, and said, "Time and events have proven our friendship and, more importantly, loyalty to each other, and I would put my life in your hands anytime. In fact, it would be impossible for me to imagine the prosperity of the Faraaz nation without you."

Haghdar stated that the prince was the only brother he had ever known, a fine brother who risked his kingdom by staying with him and suffering equally when he was down. How could he ever think of not giving his life for him? Haghdar continued that the king had no worries when it came to the friendship and loyalty between him and the prince, the only family he grew up with and fought against enemies together and stayed together through the humps and troughs of life, two brothers who were willing to make ultimate sacrifice for one another over and over again.

The king smiled and said, "Then it is done."

The next day, the king called upon the top generals, priests, and ministers to announce his succession. The king declared it was time to begin the succession process. He continued that he had no doubt about the loyalty and trustworthiness of his subjects. He affirmed considering his succession by a council consisting of members of his highly trusted top generals, ministers, and priests, with the prince and Haghdar seated as the head of the council. Alas, he did not believe that such a council would be able to serve the Faraaz nation's best interest because of the size and variety of members. Such a council, if and when established, must include representatives of different countries and nations, all of which were equal members of the Faraaz nation. Because of the empire's devotion to freedom, there were many different religious groups, ethnicities, and races, all citizens of the great nation of Faraaz who would require to be represented within such a council. Therefore, he had decided for the prince to take over the throne with Haghdar cogoverning. He ordered the prince and Haghdar to organize the high council as discussed and to concur with them regarding decisions affecting the Faraaz nation, but the final decision would be that of the prince and Haghdar.

The court members bowed before the king and proceeded toward the prince and Haghdar to express their obedience and loyalty. The king smiled in satisfaction and ordered seven days and seven nights in celebration of the crowning of the next king.

The affairs of the country and court advanced as planned, and seven months later, the king passed.

CHAPTER THIRTY-TWO

No Conflict

Zodiak breezed down the mountain and went directly to the temple of Mantik. He entered the temple and observed that the temple was overly crowded, being the only sanctuary for many outlaws. The priest was full of joy seeing Zodiak. He presumed that Zodiak's return meant he would honor his promise to defeat and conquer Fars and thereafter make him the king of the world. The priest held him in his arms and said he knew he was the promised boy. He asked Zodiak to tell him every detail of his journey. He ordered food and drinks without delay and dismissed everyone else in order to talk to him alone. Zodiak briefly explained how he killed Seepar and washed himself in its blood. He said that after gaining consciousness, he realized his priorities had changed. He no longer wished to fight for his personal ambitions or sufferings for that matter. He professed to work as hard as he could to make the world a better place for everyone. He wanted to work toward healing the sufferings of the deprived and disadvantaged. He proclaimed there could only be good and better in his vision for the world. He did not wish to be a ruler any longer nor to be ruled by another. He had decided to forgive and forget whatever wrong was done to him just as long as those who did them changed their ways and concurred with his new vision for the world.

The priest thought for a few moments. He said it seemed Zodiak had changed, but not in the way he expected. In fact, he always had his doubts whether he actually went to the top of the mountain to fight Seepar. It appeared to him that Zodiak probably wandered around for all these years and lost his ambitions, his mind, his soul, and his heart. He talked and promised to act like a coward, an attribute he despised and could not stand. He called on his guards and told them to take Zodiak out of his sight and execute him outside the temple grounds as he was not worthy to be killed there. The guards grabbed Zodiak's arms and tried to carry him out, but Zodiak did not move. The guards found him too heavy and stable; they could not move him.

The priest ordered the guards to finish him even if they had to do it in front of him. One of the guards struck Zodiak's chest with his sword as hard as he could. To everybody's surprise, the sword broke on impact, but Zodiak's chest was not even scratched. Several guards struck him with their swords and lances, but they could not pierce his skin either, and their weapons broke upon contact with his body. No weapon could penetrate Zodiak's skin from the top of his head to the tip of his toes. The priest recognized Zodiak's story was truthful. He must have killed Seepar and washed himself in its blood; hence, he could not be killed. He screamed at the guards to stop. He called on Zodiak with a smile in his eyes and on his face and claimed that was just a test. The priest continued that he had to test him to make sure he was telling the truth because cleaning the world of the agents of darkness was not an easy task and required immortality. Zodiak proved to him he was invincible, and nothing could kill him now and forever.

He then pretentiously affirmed Zodiak's vision of the new world order and wished to offer his services for such a noble and profound purpose. Zodiak had felt strength and maturity since killing Seepar but did not know he became invincible until now. He avowed the priest was a wise man and welcomed him to his camp. They must start their work without further delay. The priest suggested to rest that night and start their new journey early the next morning. Zodiak was not tired at all but accepted his offer. The priest declared,

"Let it be known to all men that Zodiak might not die or be killed. He is the savior of the world and guardian of the telling of the god of light for eternity."

That night the priest stayed up most of the night, planning. He thought that in order to change the world as Zodiak wished, he would have to kill many people. There were too many agents of darkness whose ways were theft, murder, and taking by force. They not only served the gods of darkness but also personally enjoyed violence and would not, under any circumstances, change. They would prefer to die than change their ways of living. That meant many wars, which in turn meant killing upon killing by the hands of Zodiak. And the victory belonged to Zodiak since he could not be killed and he would not die. He would never be tired, hungry, or thirsty. He could eat if he wanted to but alternatively could live for a long time without food or water. He could fight against other armies single-handedly and defeat them. Zodiak would fight and kill if he believed it was helping him to achieve his goal of changing the world for better. All he had to do was to convince Zodiak the others were bad people serving the gods of darkness. That did not appear to be such an impossible task to accomplish. It was only a matter of perception and judgment, and he could provide both of them for Zodiak. He reckoned fighting was in Zodiak's blood, something Zodiac was born and lived with for all his life and still did not recognize about himself. But the priest knew he had it in him—an inherent attribute that could be provoked without much effort. The world was full of bad people—yes, more than enough. After all, he had the boy in the palm of his hand. He would prove to Zodiak, truthfully in case of the first few instances, that the world was full of bad people. Once he gained his trust, he could simply convince him that anybody he did not approve of was bad, not worthy of his noble ideology, and therefore against him. Allowing those people to live would be contrary to his vision. They would cause trouble, insecurity, and doubts. They would convince others to go against Zodiak's vision, and the world would remain as it was as long as there was even one agent of the darkness in existence. In the course of rendering his faithful services to Zodiak, he could then easily identify these agents of the darkness and present them to Zodiak for proper punishment—death. Any movement he found contrary to his interest or even suspicious of being against his interest or any spoken word he did not approve of would be answered with death. And it was Zodiak who did the killing—an immortal executioner in his service. What a noble idea of his own.

The priest thought that soon the people of the world would realize they had only two choices—either obey him or be killed by the hands of Zodiak just as long as he held his trust. Yes, any means to attain and maintain Zodiak's trust was not out of the picture just as long as he achieved his goal. The cause, in this case, justified the means. After all, he was only a few small steps away from his lifelong dream—conquering Fars and ruling the world. The thought of ruling the world gave him a heartwarming feeling, the likes of which he had not felt since he lost his three sons. He fell asleep with these thoughts.

The next day, early in the morning, the priest woke up and found Zodiak preparing for departure. The priest said he would accompany Zodiak, but the others would be better off staying in the temple until they found a suitable place for them. All these people were wanted by the law and, once out of the temple, would be arrested and mostly executed. Even immortal Zodiak might not be able to save all of them, and therefore, their lives would be wasted. Further, they would impair their reputation, and therefore, it would be more difficult to convince the general public of their grand ideas if they were accompanied by murderers and thieves. He continued that he believed that would be against their mission. Zodiak agreed, and the two of them left the temple. The priest said, as Zodiak knew, he was not to leave the temple; his head was wanted by the law too. Zodiak said he did not have to be concerned with that. He would protect him. The priest smiled and expressed his gratitude.

As they were riding, the priest suggested changing the world for the better required some discipline and organization. They could talk to people one at a time or gather groups, but usually the public either would not believe them or, if they did, might change their minds under everyday life's ordinary pressure. Remember that the agents of darkness also were preaching to the public to encourage them to join

Ahreman. And as evidenced by their accomplishments, they were not doing a bad job. Many of the agents of darkness were in uniform and would disrupt their activities. They needed some kind of systemic organization to fend the agents of darkness and dispense their own ideology. Zodiak was listening quietly. He had thought about it himself but wanted to hear the priest's opinion. The priest continued that they needed some kind of establishment. He had created such an establishment out of outlaws and bandits, albeit those people had nowhere else to go, and in a way, he not only kept them away from hurting innocent public in general but also, to a certain degree, saved their lives. Now, however, things were completely different. They needed to have a place for all the people to come together and learn the good ways of living, one in harmony, without hate or greed, to work for the good of everyone and not only some superiors.

There should not exist any social class created by force. All would have the same chance to work and enjoy life. Superiority would be only by the way one acted toward and treated others. Wealth would be the result of creativity and innovation to improve the lives of beings and not to accumulate for personal pleasure. They must teach others to live as a commune and not as individuals. But how? Where? Zodiak answered that he had an idea—Toufan, his land and the land of his ancestors being ruled by Fars now. Toufan people were spiritually free, and although being treated relatively equitably by the establishments of Fars, they did not enjoy the freedom of ruling their own country. They deserved better. The priest smiled and whispered, "Toufan. Yes, I had heard about Toufan and in fact had exchanged some letters with the king of Toufan before he was defeated and killed by Haghdar, Fars's top general. He killed the king, husband of the queen Shahrara."

Zodiak's heart plunged at the priest's statement. He remembered his mother's words that his real mother was Shahrara, queen of Toufan, killed by some Fars generals. So Haghdar actually might have killed his father and mother. That was the reason his mother told him he would become king someday. He was to be the king of Toufan except his parents were killed by Haghdar. And that was the reason Fars generals wanted to kill him too, the true heir to Toufan's throne.

Blood rushed to his head with these thoughts. He wanted to scream. He thought he could find and kill Haghdar in the blink of an eye when heard the priest again. Haghdar was the greatest warrior who ever lived. Many believed he was invincible too. He had been severely injured many times, wounds that would have killed any warrior. But not him. Every time he became stronger and healthier. Zodiak must avoid him for now until his strength and wisdom was fully developed. It could be sometime before the powers of Seepar fully flourished in him.

He then took out of his pouch the letter he had received in the temple from the rulers who had correspondence with the king of Toufan and handed it to him. Zodiac held the letter in his hand as if it were his father's hands. He closed his eyes for a second to absorb his father's energy. Zodiak did not say a word and slowly opened his eyes again to read the letter. But the priest saw Zodiak's reaction and realized he had hit a nerve but did not know what it was. He knew he was doing everything right. It simply came so naturally to him. How exciting.

The king of Toufan had written he was displeased by the Fars generals' activities and taking of Toufan's best of the young, soldiers, and horses, and such activities must be stopped one way or another. Zodiak read the letter, and the words of his mother came to his mind again. So Fars's top generals, led by Haghdar, killed Toufan's king and then poisoned his mother, Shahrara. He also remembered having promised his mother not to tell anybody about his true identity. He was full of rage from all their brutality but calmed himself and stated that many wrongdoings took place in the past, but they were to remedy all of them and eliminate the agents of darkness, be it message or man. The priest recognized Zodiak's rage, smiled in bitterness, and quietly said, "We surely should."

CHAPTER THIRTY-THREE

JOURNEY

Zodiak and the priest decided to mostly travel at night and rest during the day to avoid problems mainly because the priest was wanted by the law. They hunted and prepared food and rested during the day and traveled most of the night. After a few days, they arrived at the border posts of Mantik and Fars. Some soldiers stopped them and asked where they were going and what their business was. The priest claimed they were merchants on their way to Toufan to buy some horses. One of the lieutenants suspected his statement and decided to search their belongings. As he was searching inside the priest's pouch, he found the letter from the king of Toufan. He recognized the priest was the king of Mantik and ordered his arrest. Zodiak interfered and told the lieutenant he better leave him alone. The lieutenant ordered his arrest as well. As the soldiers surrounded them, one of them threw his spear at the priest since the king's order was to kill him on sight anywhere outside the temple. Zodiak extended his hand in front of the spear. The spear hit his hand and broke without any injury to Zodiak's hand. In a matter of seconds, the soldiers drew their swords and attacked them. Zodiak knew they could not harm him, but they could kill the priest. He shouted at the soldiers to stop, but they were receiving orders from the lieutenant to attack. Zodiak had no choice but to defend the priest who was shaking out of fear for his life. Zodiak told the priest to stay close to him. Zodiak did not wish to harm or kill the soldiers, but the soldiers were aggressive and wanted to kill both of them. Some soldiers tried to push their swords into his heart, but their swords broke on impact without any injury to him. The soldiers could not believe their eyes. They made another attempt to kill Zodiak but to no avail. Their swords and spears could not pierce his skin. A few of the soldiers were badly injured, and the lieutenant decided to bring in reinforcements. Some hundred soldiers surrounded Zodiak and the priest. Zodiak told them he did not wish to harm them. He shouted at the soldiers to step back and let them continue their journey, and nobody would get hurt. The lieutenant ordered them to attack. Zodiak reluctantly defended the priest and injured or killed many soldiers. Eventually, the lieutenant ordered the soldiers to retreat and let them go to avoid more injuries or fatalities. Zodiak shouted that if they made any attempt to kill the priest, he would come back and kill all of them; just stay away. The priest smiled and thanked Zodiak. He felt one step closer to his goal. Once the killing started, it could not be stopped. The sequence of events was progressing exactly according to his plans, a very promising little fight that made things possible. He knew Zodiak would have to kill again sooner rather than later.

They continued their journey, but the priest suggested traveling off roads in order to avoid further problems. It was not that he cared for the others being killed by Zodiak; instead he thought it was too early for him to be recognized as a superpower. He needed more time to conquer some countries and raise an army worthy enough to fight against Fars and especially Haghdar. He knew killing some ten or twenty soldiers single-handedly was not an extraordinary challenge for Haghdar. In fact, in some wars, he had killed thousands all by himself.

So they traveled all night and camped the next day. Zodiak hunted a small deer, and the priest barbequed some meat. As they were eating, the priest said they needed to gradually draft some soldiers, train them highly, and raise a small yet very effective and capable army. The army was needed to defend their ideology and to provide land, shelter, and other necessities to spread his word. He declared there were two ways to conquer nations—one was by force and the other by way of respect and admiration. However, there was only one way to rule.

Zodiak agreed. The priest continued the king of Fars and Haghdar originally adhered to such policies except when their interest was on the line. That made them vulnerable, and in case events got tougher than they could handle, they would not hesitate to slip into the side of the darkness as they did when they killed the king of Toufan. But Zodiak did not have their weaknesses. He could not be killed and would not die and with his wisdom; they would never go to the side of the darkness. The priest then smiled and continued, "Is there not so much truth in these statements?"

The priest knew he was getting closer to his long-pursued goal by the minute. He said, nevertheless, they must always face the facts, and one was that they might have to fight the agents of darkness and, if necessary, kill them, as evidenced by what just happened the other day. Zodiak said he knew, but he preferred to avoid killing. The priest said he wished there was a way. He continued that the only weak link in their ideology was finding the way to enlighten the agents of the gods of darkness by the goodness of the god of light without having to fight them or, even worse, to kill them. But even the god of gods, the god of light, could not have found a resolution to that dilemma. They surely were not above the god of light, or Zodiak believed he was. Zodiak replied, "I am only immortal and not a god. Let us not to forget that." The priest said he never did but, for a second there, thought maybe Zodiak did. The priest then said it was with great relief he was assured of that fact even though Zodiak came as close to God as they had ever come. Besides, it was the nature of humans to believe in God as beyond man's comprehension. If they ever saw God, they would lose faith and then would make every effort to destroy it to prove they were able to overcome a fake god. It makes them feel worthy even if it is just for a moment in their melancholy thoughts—that is if they did not lose their lives on the route to such a false objective.

Zodiak said, "You need to rest before the night casts its darkness when our journey resumes." The priest closed his eyes and, before long, spread the wings of his aspirations and took to the skies of his madness.

CHAPTER THIRTY-FOUR

HOMELAND

Zodiak and the priest found their way to Toufan. Zodiak decided to first go to his hometown, where his mother was buried—a small town far away from civilization with not many changes since he left. Most other children he grew up with had already left for big cities in search of work, fame, and for some, power and wealth. They came to the grave of Zodiak's mother, which was pretty much washed away by rain and storm. Zodiak knelt before his mother's grave with the priest a step behind him. Both men dropped their heads somberly. Zodiak quietly said, "Mother, I am so sorry, so sorry that words may not express my sadness. I would give everything I have, my immortality and my life, just to be with you once again." He could not control himself and started sobbing.

The priest took a step forward and knelt next to Zodiak. He whispered, "It is the greatest honor to be here with Zodiak, your son. I carry the regrets of a thousand men not having the opportunity to meet such an eloquent and wise mother who raised a son like Zodiak—a man of vision and power who downplays his abilities to save others, a savior of humanity and human beings. Let it be known to all men that after prevailing over the agents of darkness, the greatest temple will be built here in memory of Zodiak's mother for all men to come and pay their respects to such a decent person whose teachings save men from themselves for an eternity of time.

That I promise for as long as I live." The priest then put his arm over Zodiak's wide shoulders and cried with him. Zodiac felt the sincerity of the priest's touch and realized he had a friend, his first one since childhood.

Zodiak and the priest decided to remain in the village for a short stay to plan for the future and possibly some recruits. The priest indicated it would be best if he walked around the village and talked to some people to obtain information before revealing Zodiak's true identity to the public. He warned that they should be cautious because even though Zodiak was immortal, he could be captured or trapped and kept in chains. They needed to plan their future very carefully in order to raise an army as discussed previously. Who knew? They might even get lucky and draft some talent there, as small a village as it was. Nonetheless, talent might be found anywhere. If they found talent, they might stay longer; otherwise, they would move to the next little town on their way to bigger places.

Zodiak agreed, and therefore the priest walked around the village, talking to people to maybe find some information and recruits. He did not anticipate much but thought it was a starting point.

The priest walked about the village, looking for the young, unfulfilled, and dissatisfied—especially those who were disparate, those to whom life had not offered much despite their ambitions. After a while, he came to some youngsters standing in the street corner, apparently doing nothing, waiting for nothing, and expecting nothing. He opened a conversation with them, asking some phony address. One of them, appearing to be the strongest of them all, said such an address did not exist in that village. The priest said, "Such is your life, all of you. What future address would you have standing in the street all day doing nothing? None. Absolutely nonexistence." He told them his time had passed, but there was still time for the young and strong to attain some aspiration—the kind of quality life the Fars commanders and generals enjoyed. And why should the generals prosper with the fruits of their country and their lives? Their happiness was at the cost of misery for tens of thousands of Toufanians.

The youngster sarcastically responded, "And you are the man to show our future address."

The priest claimed, "And more if you are worthy." If they were accepted by his general and joined them, they would force the Fars governors out of Toufan. They could take their fate in their own hands to serve their own country and to enjoy the fruits of their endeavors.

The young man said, "You talk big for a ragged old man. Where is this general of yours?"

The priest said, "Follow me."

The leader of the young men told his friends, "Let us follow the crazy old man. He might have something of value, and we could take it away from him." He was obviously from out of town, and they could get rid of him afterward without anybody even noticing.

So the youngsters followed the priest and he brought them to the place Zodiak was resting. However, before entering the place, the priest told them to wait outside. He entered the room alone. He explained to Zodiak the incident in the village and that he directed the youngsters there for his evaluation. They seemed to have potential, but Zodiak's opinion was essential. The priest called on the youngsters, and they entered the room, expecting to find some valuables. The instant they entered the room, they saw Zodiak sitting on a chair. Zodiak stood up to greet them. The youngsters were stunned by the sheer size and physicality of him. They had never seen anybody like him. Not only Zodiak's height, but his picturesque muscles were as if portrayed cell by cell. Zodiak looked so perfect as if he descended from gods. Young men had heard about Haghdar and thought it was him. They thought Haghdar had heard their complaints about the village's low life, that Fars only took and did not give any, not in their village anyway, and came to punish them. Afraid for their lives, they knelt before him, and their leader said, "We did not know the great Haghdar was here. We beg for forgiveness." Zodiak took the hand of their leader and told him to stand up. Zodiak told them he was not Haghdar. He continued that Toufan's young men should be brave and alarmed to make a stand for their freedom, to liberate their country from the ruling of foreigners and invaders, including but not limited to Fars and its generals. He noted that they acted like small-time thieves wasting their time on the streets or, worse, looking for an old man to mug. And when confronted with their crime, they wept like a miserable, deceptive old woman and begged for mercy. There was no hope for them.

The leader of the youngsters pulled himself together and said they wanted to be somebody. They knew about their ancestors and their bravery, but Haghdar was above man. Nobody dared to look him in the eye. In fact, he killed the king of Toufan with his own hands, the bravest, strongest, and wisest king Toufan had ever had. There was no hope for Toufan or any other nation as long as Haghdar lived, and he seemed to have an eternal life. He was invincible.

Zodiak looked him in the eye. He paused for a few seconds. The memory of Haghdar killing his father made blood run to his head. He had enough rage and anger to kill the young man right there and then. He took a deep breath and, as calmly as possible, said, "Is that so?" Haghdar was a man, just a man like them. And he was not invincible. He could be killed, and so be it if that was the only way to free Toufan and the world from his audacity in crime and murder. However, unless they were ready to change, a fundamental change to their mind-set and their ways of living, they would not be able to overcome anybody, let alone Haghdar. They must be willing to learn and make sacrifices. They must give everything they had, their time, strength, mind, and soul and everything else if necessary in order to snap out of the dirt they lived in even if it was at the cost of their lives and that of their loved ones. The young men held their heads down. Their leader said they understood what wasteful lives they had and were more than willing to join Zodiak to improve their lives and the lives of their loved ones and countrymen. They swore with their lives to follow Zodiak to the end of the world without question just as long as he helped them to be stronger in mind and in body, to show them the way to glory once bequeathed to their ancestors. They prayed to Zodiak to accept and train them to become men of honor and strength just like their fathers were.

The priest declared they must be taught the profound ideals for which Zodiak strived. They must be trained to be strong both in body and mind, especially mentally because they were to raise an army of mind over body, a contrast to the Fars army. The priest told them to go to the village and call on as many young men and women as they could. They would soon have the selection process started. Those who were accepted must be willing to make the ultimate sacrifice for the ultimate reward, both in this world and the other.

As their fundamental lessons, all new recruits had to go through Zodiak teachings first and, depending on their ability to comprehend and apply his philosophy, would be assigned to a suitable task. Those who showed serious progress would be trained to became liberators.

So the young and brave of Toufan joined Zodiak and the priest one by one. They were taught his ideals, to make a stand for their honor and to free their country from the occupation of the Fars army and its generals. Soon enough masses united with Zodiak and the priest, enough to start educating and training a small yet extremely effective army.

Zodiak and the priest delegated different tasks to different individuals; they were mostly assigned to military school. Nonetheless, some started cooking, cleaning, and many other tasks. The priest was very efficient in organization since he used to be a king. Zodiak taught them his profound ideals, the logic of the teachings of the god of light and darkness and how to find peace within. He taught them to trust their own feelings yet must control them. Their feelings would enable their logic to fly if and only if they could control them and derive positive energy from them. He explained to them that if they wanted to win over another, they must be able to win over themselves first, and that was only possible by dispersing low-level morals such as fear, anger, and hatred. These low morals would cause much negative energy, which in turn would lead them to their defeat and demise. He taught them fear, jealousy, and greed, the lowest level of morals, caused hatred, hatred sought revenge, and revenge was the tool of the gods of darkness. Revenge was the shortest way to anger, and where anger entered through the door, wisdom and logic flew out of the window.

Zodiak gradually raised a small army of philosopher warriors. Toufan was rising again and this time led by an invincible philosopher. Not even Haghdar held such quality.

CHAPTER THIRTY-FIVE

SHAKE UP

Zodiak's followers were committed to give all to their cause, be it time, money, and even their lives. Among the recruits were some with blacksmith and other industrial talents who worked in the shop and produced whatever tools they needed, including but not limited to artillery. They worked as hard as they could to prove themselves equal to militants, and that made Zodiak and the priest contented. Zodiak and the priest saw the ray of hope in their eyes and hearts. They were not only working; they were also building necessary tools and equipment to force the Fars generals out of their country. They were making a profound statement of devotion, commitment, and aspiration.

Zodiak and the priest chose a place far away from civilization as their domicile to train troops and to conduct their activities appropriately and to avoid interruption or involvement by the Fars generals and their army.

After a while, the Fars generals ruling that remote region of Toufan noticed that the best of the young population had joined a priest in a nowhere land and therefrom formed some kind of gang or sect. It seemed they kept it to themselves because there were no complaints of theft or crime; maybe some kind of lunatic sect. Nonetheless, they were concerned since strong, talented, and industrious young men and women joined the gang in masses instead of entering the labor market and eventually serving them. The labor market was getting tight, and prices were moving up. Further, the activities of this newly organized gang were not disclosed to them; they did not obtain any permit for their activities and did not establish any sort of communication with Fars authorities. Although the gang lived in a nowhere land far away from any city or civilization, they affected the cheap labor force and drove overall prices higher. They were indirectly diminishing the generals' quality of life. Moreover, their spies reported some protests by younger people who spoke of the lack of primary needs while the Fars generals enjoyed a lucrative lifestyle. They showed frustration and dissatisfaction about the manner their community was managed and demanded equitable opportunities as citizens of the Faraaz nation. Not receiving any favorable response, these individuals were joining the priest's sect in increasing numbers.

The generals held a meeting to discuss the matter and to adopt a proper resolution to their dilemma. They concluded that the gang was no match for professional soldiers of the Fars army. There was no need to report such a minor event to the king. They decided it would be best to teach this gang a lesson. They affirmed that the king naturally expected them to be able to independently maintain order against revolt by a gang. They did not wish to let the king know about their lofty ways of living at the cost of those peasants. The king might not approve of their policies, and under no circumstances did they aspire for the king's dissatisfaction.

Therefrom, they summoned one thousand of the most cruel and brutal warriors in their army to go to that part of their territory and, once and for all, establish law and order. Their explicit order was to quickly and quietly disperse the gang, get rid of their leaders, particularly the priest, and destroy their camp in order to force survivors, if any, to go back to their villages and enter the labor markets, where the best of them would be employed by the general's recruiters, an employment slightly above slavery. The remaining, if any, would either be left alone to die in their misery or taken as slaves.

Shortly thereafter, Fars troops were mobilized toward Zodiak's camp. Their captain had fought along Haghdar in different wars and was notorious for brutality and cruelty.

They marched through cities and villages without much resistance. Ordinary citizens did not dare to face the Fars army, especially those warriors who were known for their viciousness. Facing no resistance and, in some villages, being greeted by the locals made them overly confident, and they lamely marched toward their destination. The captain of the troops joked that they were going to some kind of picnic instead of a fight. Most nights the captain and his lieutenants drank and enjoyed the best of Toufan's women on their route to the supposedly party finale.

Meanwhile, Zodiak received news about Fars's army mobilization and initially thought that could serve as a test of the abilities of his young army. As agreed with the priest, he had not said a word to anybody about being invincible, and the priest was the only person to know about it. As the head of their organization's hierarchy, the priest had produced a council consisting of the best of the best of their warriors, thinkers and strategists similar to that of Mantik; loyal subjects who shared his vision and were willing to carry his orders no matter of the danger, ambitious young blood in his newly formed army.

The priest and Zodiak privately met to discuss fast-approaching Fars battalion before talking to the council. The priest suggested that Zodiak's abilities must not be spoken of. He believed it was too early for them to enter an all-out war with Fars. Zodiak agreed, and they both remained tight lipped. The priest indicated that in case the battle with Fars's battalion became inevitable, Zodiak's invincibility would be uncovered but even then must not be spoken of. They needed every second before the news scattered around the Faraaz nation.

They then called on the council to deliberate the forthcoming incident and to seek their wisdom. The meeting was held immediately, chaired by the priest, to hash out a strategy to deal with the Fars army. They received information about the Fars troops' structure and knew that those hurtful warriors were not to tolerate or negotiate terms. They knew the troops particularly aimed at them. They did not kill any other on their way. They were to destroy and kill them, possibly take the young and strong as slaves at best. The priest weighed in that they must do whatever was necessary to prevent war with the Fars army. He continued that win or lose, they would be at serious risk if the battle started. If they won, Fars would send an army the size and ability of which has not been heard of in history. Such a vast and powerful army would surely be headed decisively by Haghdar himself. They were no match for Haghdar; not even Zodiak was prepared to fight him. And in case they lost, the Fars army would kill all ranks and files and take the rest as slaves. They would be finished either way. It was an impossible situation, one that could soon put an end to their ideals, hard work, and the freedom of Toufan. They discussed surrendering but reasonably came to conclusion that this division of the Fars army would not settle with anything less than killing the leaders, more specifically the priest, Zodiak, and the council alongside the old and sick. They would chain the young and strong and take them as slaves—if for no other reason, to make an example of them as show of power and a lesson of force to others.

Zodiak articulated that then there was really no way out of the fight. They could defeat the army of one thousand and live to see the light of another day. The priest agreed but added that upon the destruction of the Fars army, they would have no choice but to get into the final stage of freeing Toufan in a hurry, a move much earlier than they had planned for. The Fars army would come after them sooner rather than later. Time would run fast, and they should too. They must get into battle mode and raise an army suitable to fight Haghdar before he got to them. Zodiak uttered that they were a mobile community and could fight smaller rulers, recruit those warriors willing to join them, and move on to the next territory. Because of their relatively small numbers and quick mobility, they could be hard to catch up with. In other words, they could raise the army on the road. The priest injected that when it came to mobility, no army could escape that of Fars. They were enormous, but their advanced technology afforded them to be faster than one could say goodbye. However, they had no other choice. The Fars army was getting dangerously close. The council contemplated that there would be many casualties but still preferred that over total destruction. The priest said, "Then let us take this show on the road." The council agreed.

The council continued their meeting to draft plans to confront the Fars battalion. They decided to initially send an envoy consisting of the oldest man in the camp and his youngest daughter to hopefully deter the Fars army from attacking the camp. They were not very optimistic about the outcome of the negotiation, if any, but that would give rise to an opportunity for some warriors to reach behind the Fars troops without being noticed and then surround them. The priest suggested that in case they fought, no Fars soldier should live. They could not afford to allow even one of the Fars militants to go back and give the news to the generals, which would be a matter of few days. If they were all killed, it would be few weeks before the Fars generals found out their army was completely destroyed. That would afford them some time to pack and leave. Zodiak took helm of the leadership and gave his warriors final instructions. He decided to ride in front and middle of the troops to meet with the Fars army in case negotiations were not fruitful. Overall there were seven hundred people in the camp, out of whom less than five hundred were warriors, more than enough for him to defeat one thousand Fars soldiers.

CHAPTER THIRTY-SIX

First Cut

The Fars army arrived some seven kilometers outside the camp, where the old man and his daughter were waiting for them. The old man and his young daughter approached the Fars captain with a white piece of cloth in her hand. The captain ordered the troops to stop. The old man greeted the captain and inquired about his intentions. He said there was a rumor that the great Fars army was marching against his camp, the underlying reason of which was unknown to him and his people. He continued that these were peaceful men and women with no ambitions except to live calmly and do about with their own lives. They were no danger to anybody and only pursued peace in solitude on this faraway land.

The captain responded, "Listen carefully, old man, because I am going to say this only once. Go back to your camp and tell everybody, every man, woman, and child, to stand in line. Some will perish, and those lucky enough to live will be taken as slaves. You have four hours to comply. We will march on the fifth hour, and if so, all will be disposed of. Now go as the winds of time already began to blow." The old man thanked the captain for his generosity to allow him and his daughter to leave alive and went back to the camp.

Meanwhile, some hundred Toufanian warriors had reached behind the Fars army as planned by Zodiak. He left some hundred warriors in the camp in case they had to retreat, some one hundred disguised and hid on the left, and another hundred on the right side of the battleground in a relatively narrow passage through low hills two kilometers outside their camp. He rode with one hundred warriors in the middle and out.

The Fars army rested for two hours and then began marching toward the camp. As they arrived two kilometers before the camp, they were confronted with Zodiak and his warriors. The Fars army, consisting of experienced professional soldiers, realized they had to fight their way into the camp, which they thought was not a problem. Both sides were prepared to destroy the other completely. As Zodiak came closer, the captain noticed his size and strength. For a second, he thought he was Haghdar. He could not believe his eyes. As they came closer to one another, the captain realized Zodiak must be their leader and therefore called on some hundred soldiers and instructed them to only fight Zodiak. He ordered them not to be concerned about any other warrior because if they killed him, the rest would run for their lives and subsequently could be chased and killed.

The battle took only few short hours. Those hundred soldiers took aim at Zodiak but could not kill him. Zodiak cut through them like hot knife through butter. Several of them pushed their spears or swords into his heart, but none could pierce his skin. Some of his warriors also noticed Zodiak was not even injured, not even a scratch on his skin, and as the battle advanced, he became stronger and faster. It seemed as if Zodiak did not need any warrior to help him and was able to single-handedly defeat the Fars army. The captain of the Fars army ordered the soldiers to retreat, but the Toufan warriors blocked their way from behind, and Zodiak quickly killed the entire battalion. Not even one Fars soldier was left alive. Casualties were minimal among Zodiak's warriors, and injuries similarly were few. Almost all the warriors came back to the camp. Many of them did not even draw their weapons. They just watched Zodiak destroying the Fars army all by himself.

Upon returning to the camp, Zodiak met with the priest. The priest was exceedingly delighted by their victory. It meant to him more than just destruction of Fars's small battalion. He was certain there was no turning point for Zodiak now that he had the blood of one thousand people on his hands. It was only a matter of time to encounter Haghdar and Fars's army.

The word about Zodiak's impregnability spread in the camp fast and raised the spirit of Toufanians. They now believed Zodiak was the promised one to bring greatness to their beloved land once again. They thought of their ancestors and their bravery and strength. They believed Toufan would rise and conquer the world once and for all.

The priest and Zodiak ordered everybody to pack, burn the camp behind them, and move out of that territory. Once the camp was burned, Zodiak rounded up everybody to render a short speech. He said, "Today was a great victory, the first of many more to come. Sooner rather than later, the Fars army, led by Haghdar himself, will pursue us once word of today's defeat travels to the king's court. However, no-one should speak of what was witnessed today with anybody. The Fars army is experienced, strong, and enormous. We are only a few hundred in number, and no matter how many Fars's soldiers we killed, there would be more to come." Accordingly, he and the priest compelled everyone to keep his secret until the proper moment arrived. They must keep quiet in this regard if they wanted to succeed to recoup their country. They all avowed to secrecy and followed Zodiak and the priest to their next destination.

CHAPTER THRITY-SEVEN

THE NEWS

The Fars generals anxiously were waiting for the troops to come back with the heads of the priest and other leaders of the gang and, of course, many young men and women slaves. Nonetheless, no message had come from the troops since the day before they had reached the priest's camp. After waiting for several days with anxiety, they decided to dispatch the spies in order to find out about the status of the mission. After a few days, the spies returned and brought the bad news. The Entire battalion was killed, and the priest and his followers disappeared. Not even one militant survived. Further, there was a rumor about the priest's first general and leading warrior being invincible. He promised to revive Toufan's greatness. He pledged to bring back to Toufan what was said in the legends but lost since being defeated by Fars. He had avowed to defeat Fars and particularly kill Haghdar with his own hands. He intended to deliver the Faraaz throne to the priest as the new king. He lifted the people's spirit, and they believed in this individual wholeheartedly. There were also rumors that he single-handedly annihilated the Fars battalion of one thousand.

The generals hurriedly conjured a meeting and came to the decision to immediately inform the king of Fars of this grand scheme. They sent their fastest messenger to Fars, emphasizing the need for Haghdar himself to impede this warrior before it was too late.

Zodiak and his followers rushed to nearby villages and cities one after another, destroyed Fars troops, and asked Toufanians to join them. Toufanians, being suppressed by Fars generals, put their faith and courage in Zodiak's hands. They all pledged their lives to support him in order to bring back greatness to Toufan, to liberate her, and to establish the most free and virtuous empire the world had ever seen, one to surpass Fars.

Zodiak's popularity grew fast and far beyond what Toufan had ever experienced. Not even the previous king, Shahrara's husband, had reached such a level of admiration and recognition. Many Toufanians would willingly give their lives to just prove their loyalty to Zodiak. Toufan's women, in particular, reinvigorated their men to join him and help bring back pride and glory to their beloved country. Zodiak's victories and noble ideals reached and pierced Toufanians' heart and soul from which strength and belief stemmed and blossomed to wisdom, a nation's journey to prominence and distinction. Zodiak was the sun from which rays of hope and pride, wisdom, and bravery shed on all of Toufan land and nation. Many eminent warriors bowed to his powers upon defeat; none could harm him. Gradually, his fame coupled that of Haghdar. Toufanians believed he was the only leader who could match and win over Haghdar, and that lit the fire of confidence and courage in their hearts and souls. They were already attaining what no nation, other than Fars, had ever accomplished in such a short period of time.

The priest and Zodiak, however, were wary of their warriors. Although many brave Toufanians joined them and pledged their loyalty, having lived passively in despair without aspiration for years had destroyed their military capabilities, and therefore, intensive training was necessary to turn them into professional soldiers. They knew that victory against some local generals who basically relied on Fars's strength and did nothing other than drinking and chasing young girls was not comparable with war against Haghdar and his army. Haghdar probably could have defeated all of these Fars generals and their armies in those territories single-handedly, that was if they went to war against one another.

If Haghdar came to fight them, more likely than not, their entire personnel would be either killed or taken as slaves and, in the case of Zodiak, in particular, captured and imprisoned forever. The Fars army and especially the king and Haghdar themselves were known for their cruelty against treachery and kindness to friends. Zodiak and the priest understood they were no friends of Fars and could not expect any mercy from Haghdar.

Zodiak was mostly fretful about his warriors despite all other concerns. Toufanians were joining them faster than they had planned, and therefore, there were not enough logistics and infrastructure to support sufficient training before they entered an all-out war against Haghdar.

The priest was in charge of the organization of the fast-growing new kingdom, and considering the circumstances, in fact, he was doing a good job. New recruits would be briefed about rules and regulations and what was expected of them in the camp. All men and women would then go through different tests to be evaluated for their final task. Those men strong enough and with talent for hardware would enter the military academy and were trained quickly. The best of them then would rise in the rank and became officers in charge of new recruits.

The Toufan camp had grown in numbers and could not move as fast as they used to. The high council knew that Fars army was the most mobile military force on the planet. They could reach and surround them swiftly. Toufan needed better establishments, a country with borders, and utmost organization to generate authority and strength through systemic and standard laws, rules, and regulations.

The priest, being fully aware of the need for governing laws and following the teachings of Zodiak, shortly prepared and presented the draft of the constitutional laws to the council and Zodiak. Indeed, he had merged Zodiak's ideas with that of the Good Book and, the council affirmed it quickly with slight, if any, changes. The new constitution specifically had provisions to allow future amendments or changes as were required to cope with the changing time.

The priest also organized a fundamental military school in which not only war strategies and tactics were taught but also Zodiak's ideals and philosophy were professed. Zodiak personally taught top generals in both practical and academic subjects. Toufan was awakening and rising fast, united by constitutional laws that applied equitably to all, an ideal philosophy, unparalleled confidence, firm faith, strong love for country, and the second best, if not the best, military in the known world. The Toufanians' conviction for Zodiak was resilient and attractive to many different people, even those originally not from Toufan.

After less than a year, Zodiak thought it was time to institute his resolve in a more systematic manner by conquering a large territory, including big cities, and founded a country named New Toufan, a new powerful sovereign asserted to the world and especially Fars. Soon enough, Zodiak conquered adjoining territories ruled by Fars generals and extended the power and wealth of New Toufan close to the Fars borders.

The council and priest believed time was against them as many of them were old and might not live much longer. They were eager to see Toufan's dominance over Fars before they died. They claimed New Toufan was able to withstand the Fars military force and therefore should send a message to the king of Fars, demanding the departure of his army from the areas in Toufan that were still ruled by Fars generals, or else prepare for war. Nonetheless, Zodiak still did not think New Toufan was ready to confront Haghdar and preferred to see more progress both in civil and military fronts before communicating with Fars. He told the council they were conquering many territories and expanding both in terms of land and manpower under their ruling; hence, as long as Fars did not knock on their door, they must be patient. Contrary to the high council's opinion, he believed time was on their side.

The council and the priest collaborated with Zodiak but reminded him from time to time of their eagerness to see Fars defeated before they died. Zodiak thought their hope for victory was a good-enough motivation to keep them alive. They instituted the pillars based on which the New Toufan would free the world. Zodiak needed the council and the priest, and they more than needed him. More power to all of them.

CHAPTER THIRTY-EIGHT

THE DECISION

The generals' messengers arrived at the Fars courtyard and requested to be received by the prince, now the king of Faraaz nation, and Haghdar immediately since they were carrying a dire message. They were received upon request, and after paying their respects and the customary pleasantries, delivered the generals' message. They said the entire Faraaz nation might be in danger because of the rise of a new force in Toufan. This new force had fought Fars envoys for the last several months and killed many of the soldiers and generals. Further, they liberated slaves and released prisoners upon defeating Fars governors and their armies. Subsequent to their freedom, the slaves and prisoners commonly pledged allegiance to their cause. They appeared to be led by a priest, a mystery warrior, and an accommodating high council. Additionally, since they left Toufan, the priest's army led by this general, had conquered additional regions and declared independence. They avowed themselves as a sovereign country called New Toufan. The messengers uttered that New Toufan's top general, not to be of any significance compared with the great Haghdar, was said to be invincible, who single-handedly defeated armies. He not only was the utmost warrior but also professed ideals and philosophy against Fars's ruling of their nation. In fact, his exemplars were that of socialism in which all were equal, and the wealth of their nation belonged to all equitably. The priest, the high council, and their top general lived within the same means as everybody else. They did not have palaces nor ate or dressed differently from any other. Toufanians were joining them in masses, and their faith in the new nation and their leaders' preaching could not be shattered by anyone other than the king and the great Haghdar. In their message, the generals humbly prayed to the king and Haghdar to personally attend to the rising of this evil without delay as tomorrow might be late.

The king and Haghdar, sitting atop the hall on equal seats, saw and felt fear in the eyes and voices of the messengers. The king ordered messengers to be rewarded generously for their effort and dismissed. The messengers were told to go back to Toufan and await the king's special envoy to deliver royal instructions. The king and Haghdar had received reports from different sources about this new general. Many concurred he was not to be killed and could defeat armies all by himself. The reports were inconceivable, but different sources indicated the same intelligence. If, indeed, he was invincible, Fars was confronted with the utmost vital situation. The rise of this sect, if in fact the messengers' statements were true, was a greater hurdle than any other Fars had ever encountered. Particularly, this new general and his prophecy were of ultimate danger to the essence of Fars laws and beliefs. For obvious reasons, such a force would not tolerate any ideology or supremacy other than its own and therefore must be destroyed before it was too late. The problem was that they had no information about this warrior or the source of his powers other than what the reports and messengers specified.

So, they conjured the high council to discuss the pressing subject and to adopt a suitable remedy under the circumstances. The council agreed with the king and Haghdar. If this general actually had powers with which he was credited, he must be eliminated not just because he was to liberate Toufan from Fars's governance, but he might very well be aiming at conquering Fars and becoming the king of all Faraaz, almost the entire world. Moreover, his philosophy of socialism was adverse to that of the empire, where ownership of property, the most sacred commandment of the god of light, could be abolished. Hence, court subjects and servants and even slaves lived under similar conditions as the king, Haghdar, and similarly everybody else. That was if they survived. Most likely, the liberated slaves would kill them even if New Toufan's general did not.

They concluded that this warrior's ultimate objective was to possess the world individually and all to himself. Not even his followers would have the right to ownership, and if nobody else owned anything, he would own them all. Indeed, it was a frightful outcome for humanity and humankind. They resolved that this evil must be stopped one way or another. Nothing should prevail over the elimination of this monster who would not only destroy Fars but would establish the ruling of the gods of darkness for eternity. They were confronted with the rise of the gods of darkness, which the Good Book of the god of light had warned against for thousands of years. He unquestionably must be destroyed.

The council then ratified a mandate for all and any means, even at the cost of the general population's lives, to kill this agent of the gods of darkness. They recommended for the army to be mobilized and anybody who could carry a weapon, regardless of age or gender, to join the military. It was time for the entire Fars nation to serve their beloved country and god.

The darkest age was about to be cast over Fars and over all humanity. For Fars, this wager could not be more critical. For humanity, it was the war of thousands of years between the god of light and the gods of darkness. Accordingly, it was crucial that the king and the great Haghdar commanded the military. The high council prayed for permission to accompany them to submit their wisdom in order to achieve this just cause since physical force solely could not kill this creature. It required wisdom and sacrifice by all. The council pledged their loyalty to the king and Haghdar once more and prayed to be allowed to sacrifice their lives for the good of the god of light and greatness of the Faraaz nation. It was most important, they declared, that Fars defeat and eliminate this agent of darkness. It was equally important to maintain the Faraaz nation intact because any division of it could give rise to conflict, a major source of power for the gods of darkness.

The high priests suggested to attend the temple of the god of light first to pray and seek wisdom. They inserted that it was time for the god of light and the gods of darkness to settle their eternal conflict. The burden of such a life-or-death endeavor was on the shoulders of all faithful and believers of the teachings of the god of light and not only the king and the great Haghdar.

The king and Haghdar agreed with most of their recommendations except that the king's first son would be seated as the king with the high council as chancellors while they led the army. The young prince needed the high council's wisdom until they saved the world from this vile agent once and for all and returned to Fars victoriously.

The king and Haghdar went to the temple of the god of light accompanied by the high council to seek wisdom and peace within before taking on the mission. Haghdar then went to Raad and briefed it. Haghdar told Raad that the two of them had participated in and led the Fars military to many wars. There were small enemies and large ones, but they always relied on and trusted each other, and that was the major reason for their triumphs. Nonetheless, now they had to engage in the greatest war there ever was and ever would be. They must defeat and kill what could not be killed. They had fought many indispensable warriors and enemies, but this one was different. This agent must have been receiving his powers directly from the gods of darkness. A win or loss would write the future course of humanity for an unforeseeable future. The god of light defeated and exiled the gods of darkness thousands of years ago, but now the darkness was rising again, gaining powers beyond what they had seen or experienced in the past. Regardless of Fars's victory or defeat, this might well be the war from which they would not come back. Raad lifted its head and shoulders and looked at Haghdar straight in the eyes for what seemed to be forever, then it softly pushed Haghdar with its head and knelt for him to saddle up and ride. Haghdar understood Raad; if they were going to die, better be with dignity and pride. There was no time for pity. It was the time for acting wisely and with authority. History was being written, and they were determined to be on the winning side and not necessarily the living.

Soon after, Fars assembled the largest army the world had ever known, with Haghdar and the king on the helm on their way to settle an ancient conflict, the final battle between the god of light and the gods of darkness. They knew the gods of darkness, upon defeat, would rise again, but not for another thousand years.

The people of Fars grasped the severity of the troops' movement. They had not seen a war when both the king and Haghdar convoyed the entire army ever since the king's father died. Thus, they felt grave danger, one that could change, if not end, their lives as they had known their entire lives and their ancestors had known as far as memory allowed. People lined up on the sides of the road, cheering for the king and Haghdar. They offered whatever they could to help with the stern cause and to build confidence. The sincerity of the Fars nation raised the king and Haghdar's resolve and conviction of their procuring purpose to stop and destroy agents of the gods of darkness no matter what shape or condition they were in.

The king and Haghdar campaigned during the day, studying the environment and the condition of the soldiers and commanders in order to assess their abilities, and planned at night. They were familiar with the path to Toufan and devised sophisticated strategic and tactical plans to confront the enemy in the place of their choosing. Haghdar had already fought Toufanians led by Shahrara's husband, the king of Toufan, and did not want to have the next war in the same location. The Fars army was too large in number and quantity of military equipment and gear; therefore, they needed a vast area to mobilize them. Once in their quarters, the king and Haghdar reviewed plans, maps, and the sequence of events and evaluated possible scenarios. They believed this was the most complete and efficient war blueprint they ever devised. The king and Haghdar decided to plan for the New Toufan's army to bring the war to them rather than Fars to be the aggressor. To accomplish this objective, they sent the Fars navy to the far-west waters behind the enemy lines. From there the navy was to fire upon them from the sea and push their forces toward the location where the king and Haghdar with Fars's army were waiting. The navy had to land at some point, which was upon pushing the enemy inland so far that their firepower could not reach them. The orders for the navy were to maintain distance and only fire from afar. In case enemy forces rushed back toward them, they must retreat to the ships in the sea, where they had substantial superiority and could drown them. Subsequently and dependent on the conditions of the navy's advancements, the king would send instructions outlining when and how to get involved in hand-to-hand combat. More than one thousand ships sailed, carrying well over three hundred thousand navy crews and marines. The king and Haghdar led the army of more than seven hundred thousand well-trained professional soldiers, including majority of Javidan. The sheer size and ability of Fars's military would give shivers to any warrior, including Zodiak.

The king and Haghdar knew their plans were sophisticated and beyond the comprehension of most militants, maybe even the invincible agent of the gods of darkness who was the only obstacle to guarantee firm victory. The king and Haghdar reviewed their plans over and over to make sure nothing was overlooked. One night the king abruptly asked, "How do you defeat one who may not be killed? This warrior surely would kill many Fars soldiers and, if the intelligence is true, maybe the entire army. He would never get tired, and in fact, as he fights more, he becomes stronger." The king continued that they must make all sacrifices, to the last man if necessary, in order to send this warrior and his army to the deepest part of the darkness, but that was not what he wished. The king cared about his people and army and desired to have minimal possible casualties, with which Haghdar concurred. Haghdar said that the Fars army was unmatched in all matters and levels. They had cutting-edge technology and artillery, which made them by far superior to any other military force, the likes of which world had not seen. The military personnel, every one of them, was highly trained. They were soldiers with considerable abilities, many of whom devoted their entire lives to improving their military skills. Haghdar and the king believed in the capabilities of the Fars military and the soldiers' obedience as well as their loyalty to their king and country.

Haghdar noted that they had to emphasize and rely on their strength and experience. The rest was unknown and out of their control. There was nothing else they could do other than to make sure their plans were sufficiently progressive and detailed beyond the enemies' imagination. The precise execution by each and every one of Fars's militants was equally critical. The command hierarchy had to be seamlessly effective. Haghdar added that if this agent of darkness might not be killed, he must be captured like a wild animal and kept in captivity for as long as he lived. Who knew? With a little luck, they might win and turn a determinant page of history in favor of the commandments of the god of light. The king smiled and said, "You certainly have a point there."

CHAPTER THIRTY-NINE

Preparation

Zodiak and the priest knew Fars would campaign against them and their movement any day. They liberated many of Toufan's regions as fast as possible and immediately sent new recruits to the camps for training. Zodiak was especially concerned about his people. He did not wish a massacre of his soldiers and followers. Being invincible, he was confident of his own survival and safety but knew Haghdar would not have mercy on others. He would not stop killing his people until and unless he killed him. Only then might he pardon some Toufanians, but there existed no guarantee for such a generosity in a fight between the god of light and the gods of darkness. He now strongly believed that Haghdar pretended adherence to commandments of the god of light and secretly was an agent of the gods of darkness. An imposter. He believed Haghdar received his powers from darkness. In fact, the gods of darkness must have given him all their powers since this could very well be the last confrontation between the believers of the god of light and agents of the gods of darkness for thousands of years to come. After all, Haghdar was not invincible yet prevailed every war. He had been injured many times to the point that no ordinary man would have lived; alas, he survived and came back healthier and stronger. Many warriors did not dare to look at him in the eyes; many more fled with his presence in the battlefield.

Zodiak's concern was that even though some Toufanians knew he was invincible, they still would desert the battlefield once they saw Haghdar and Raad in front of the Fars's army. Zodiak frantically talked to his people, especially his top generals, frequently and advised them to leave Haghdar to him. He insisted that he personally would fight Haghdar and bring his head; nonetheless, he had a feeling deep inside that many of the soldiers, particularly new recruits, would be too scared to fight an army led by Haghdar. He did not have any doubt about their loyalty; it was just that, except for himself, Haghdar was by far superior in body and mind over everybody else. The fear of fighting Haghdar had been engraved in their hearts and souls for decades and could not be erased overnight.

Brusquely, Zodiak and the high council received intelligence about Fars's campaign toward Toufan with the largest assembly of an army, a navy, and Javidan ever heard or seen. The king personally led Javidan and Haghdar the rest of the military. The number of Fars's soldiers was estimated to be more than one million. They carried the most advanced artillery and equipment. The reports showed that the Fars army was equipped with weapons beyond conventional wisdom. They could kill them from afar without the need for hand-to-hand combat. There were more than one thousand ships to accommodate their campaign. These ships would go around them and land militants and marines from the far west waters behind Toufan defense lines in order to surround them, Haghdar and Javidan from the front and Fars's navy from behind. It was not a pretty picture. This war was for real and not against a few drunk generals and their lame lieutenants and soldiers.

Zodiak, the priest, the high council, and the top generals held meetings regularly and discussed the impediment with which they were confronted. They decided it was time to demonstrate Zodiak's special capabilities to assure all Toufanians he could not be killed and therefore their victory was warranted. They wanted to show to Toufanian soldiers in particular this time that the Fars army and Haghdar had something to be fearful of. Truly, for a few decades, the best warriors fell to their graves by Haghdar's hands. But not this time. He was to be killed; that Zodiak promised.

They therefore rounded up the entire army the next day. Zodiak went on top of an elevated platform so everybody could see him. He shouted as loud as he could; the bad news was that Fars's army led by the king himself and Haghdar were campaigning toward Toufan. Fars had raised an army of some one million strong. They had sophisticated artillery and equipment many of which were unknown to man. They could kill many warriors from afar without the need for personal confrontation. Additionally, some one thousand ships were accommodating the Fars army. They would go around and land behind them from far west. The king led Javidan, the most dreadful murderers, and Haghdar the rest of the military. They would not have mercy on anybody, and their goal was to kill as many as they could and few survivors, if any, taken as slaves. They would do the tradition to their wives, sisters, and mothers regardless of their age and then either take them as slaves or, worse, kill them. Fars must know about Toufan's leader, Zodiak's certain abilities, and hence would be most cruel and heartless.

On the other hand, New Toufan was a coalition of some hundred thousand brave and sophisticated soldiers. Most of them joined the army for less than a year, but he had confidence in their loyalty and capabilities. They had the wise priest and high council on their side, who could afford them wisdom, faith, and support, which, considering the circumstances, were needed equally if not more. More importantly, they were fighting for their freedom and for their beloved land. New Toufan asked for nothing more than what they were entitled to—their country, which had been their land for thousands of years, dignity, independence, and respect.

Zodiak continued that he knew the most vital concern of them all was Haghdar. He was a legend, an experienced warrior who had never been defeated. Nevertheless, Toufanians must know he would be killed in this war by the hands of Zodiak. He added that Toufanians might have heard rumors about Zodiak being invincible. They could rest assured that they were not rumors. It was true. He could not be killed, and he would not die. Zodiak lauded the promise to fight to the end to either kill Haghdar or be killed by him. And Zodiak could not be killed. That left only one option. Haghdar would be killed in his unholy war.

He warned Toufan's soldiers not to allow the fear of Haghdar to overcome their bravery and courage. They must fight Fars's soldiers and leave Haghdar to him. He emphasized that they must carry his commands and avoid Haghdar no matter the situation. To prove his claim of invincibility, he took off his top clothes and asked several generals to strike him with their swords in the heart, neck, and head as hard as they could. The generals drew their swords, and each struck him with all his strength. To everybody's disbelief, their swords broke on contact but did not even scratch Zodiak's skin. The soldiers watched astonishingly with a smile on their faces. Their spirits lifted and their confidence rose. With all the artillery and apparatus Fars had, they could not hurt Zodiak, and as long as their leader was alive, they could not be defeated. They felt it was time to give Haghdar a dose of his own medicine, and Zodiak was the man to do it. They imagined themselves to soon be free, to own their land and live their own way of life without any fear. The Toufanians had no doubt about their liberator, the man promised by the Good Book of the god of light who would free them for the eternity of time. Zodiak would live forever, and Toufan would endure forever in glory, proud and dignified.

Zodiak then pronounced, "As you could see, I am invincible. I cannot be killed. I hereby guarantee that Haghdar will be killed and the Fars army destroyed." The Toufanians knelt before Zodiak; they dropped their heads in respect to observe a moment of silence. They quietly prayed to the god of light, thankful for sending Zodiak to free them. They knew Zodiak was special but now had every confidence they would prevail over and defeat Fars's ruling once and for all. They all pledged their allegiance again, genuinely believing Fars was not to defeat them—not this time, not ever again.

Zodiak felt the heavy weight on his shoulders since it was because of him that Fars was bringing the ultimate brutality and ruthlessness to the war against New Toufan. However, he believed this was the only path to independence and freedom.

CHAPTER FORTY

FIRST BATTLE

The Fars navy arrived at far west end waters of Toufan but could not see any of the enemy troops. The navy had huge catapults with which they could throw large amounts of fire to far distances, more than two kilometers. This was the weapon no man had seen before. Regular catapults could only throw rocks to short distances. Their commander ordered to fire on the shore in order to smoke them out. After practically burning whatever existed on the shore, they discharged large boats from the ships into the sea in order to land a limited number of troops and equipment. Upon landing, the marines quickly secured the shore, and the transfer of soldiers and gear, including catapults, commenced. They then started advancing cautiously. They built temporary posts from place to place and stationed soldiers there to make sure the enemy could not ambush them from behind or sink their ships. They advanced for seven days before seeing a small group of Toufanians. The Fars commander ordered to fire from afar. In a matter of minutes, fire started to pour from the skies on Toufan's troops. Those who survived started running inland. The Fars navy chased them further. After a few hours of chasing, they came to a narrow passage in between shallow hills where suddenly the grounds opened up and Toufan soldiers, who had camouflaged in the bunkers, surrounded them, and a fierce fight started. The navy commander realized they were trapped and thereupon ordered to retreat. The Toufanians were excellent archers and killed many of the marines with their arrows. The commander and a few were able to escape and go back to the nearest post.

The navy commander right away ordered all equipment on the ships to be brought to the shore and to begin advancement with full force. The commander realized the enemy was wise and brave. There was no time for any concern about the ships, and he had none. He sent a message to the king using one of his trained hawks and informed him of the situation. The message explained that they had to abandon the ships. They were likely drowned by the enemy by the time the king received the message. Therefrom, the navy was advancing eastward and might confront the enemy anytime. Some 10 percent of the navy personnel were perished by then.

The king and Haghdar received the naval commander's message. They were displeased with the first confrontation with the enemy, which resulted in the loss of some 10 percent of the navy, a huge blow to their plans. They realized there must have been some truth to the rumors they had heard about this warrior. Not only he was invincible, but he was also smart and could not be underestimated any further. The king sent a message to the commander to proceed with caution. There could be many more traps, and an unreasonable loss of personnel would not be acceptable. The king also instructed him to continue to push Toufan's army toward the battlefield of their choice but, to the extent possible, to keep their distance and avoid confrontation. No risk might be taken. Shoot first and then shoot again, the king commanded. The king required frequent reports regarding the navy's advancement.

The navy commander received the king's orders and charged the marines to start shooting fire ahead before they made advancements. There was a sea of fire a couple kilometers ahead of them at all times. To heat up the enemy, they used certain oil that would burn at a high temperature for a long time.

Their plan was to clear their path before advancing, and it was working. From time to time, Toufan's troops hiding in the bunkers in order to trap Fars's navy could not bear the fire and heat and came out to escape when the marine archers shot them with other huge catapults, shooting hundreds of poisonous arrows at the same time. The navy killed them like animals. Nonetheless, some of them were able to escape. They went back to their camp and informed Zodiak of the situation. They reported that Fars's firepower was beyond defense. The skies two kilometers ahead of the Fars navy were on fire at all times. Toufan was burning.

Zodiak held a meeting with the priest and high council to adapt a new strategy. They came to the conclusion that the only way to stop Fars's navy was from behind. However, they were more than seven days ahead of the Fars navy, and Zodiak was needed in front of the army. His absence for a period of two or three weeks could be disastrous should he go back to fight the Fars navy. On the other hand, Haghdar and the Fars army were fast approaching from the east, and in Zodiak's absence, they could finish the entire army. Fars's navy was very proficient, with more than two hundred thousand marines. Toufan's army had only less than a hundred thousand soldiers, many of them still in training. After much deliberation, Zodiak concluded that there was no alternative but to face Haghdar and the Fars army. The fact was that they learned about the size and firepower of the Fars military the hard way. They knew that eventually they would have to fight them; therefore, they had no choice but to charge eastward and attack the Fars army before the navy caught up with them from behind. Additionally, once combating Fars forces, the navy might not fire upon them because they would kill their own soldiers too. In fact, the safest place for them was the battlefield with the Fars army. Quite ironic. The closer they stayed to the hostile enemy, the better chance of victory they had. This was not what they had in mind, but it seemed to be the only way out under the circumstances. The high council reluctantly agreed and ordered the troops to immediately proceed with a faster pace.

CHAPTER FORTY-ONE

THE ARRANGEMENTS

The king and Haghdar received reports indicating the navy was finally on track, pushing the Toufan army toward the battlefield of their choosing. The Toufanians were mobilized and approaching fast. The king, Haghdar, and the Fars army had arrived at the battlefield a few days earlier. They spent all their time reviewing plans to make sure the generals and their subordinates, all the way to the frontline infantry, understood their duties. Positioning and timing was of the essence. They went over all the troops' moves with the generals several times and received and studied reports of the transition of orders throughout the command chain. They had calculated the exact date and time when Toufan's army would arrive. They reckoned the Toufanians must be tired and their strength diminished, being chased by the navy for weeks. In particular, they had to travel faster for the last several days because Fars's navy had accelerated their speed, chasing them from behind. Fars's navy moved quickly, mostly riding chariots. Heavy equipment and artillery were pulled by elephants and camels.

One major element of Fars's plan was to attack Toufan's army at first sight in order not to allow them to have a minute of rest. The battlefield of their choosing was a vast flat area. Fars had strategically camouflaged catapults and archers to surprise the Toufan army and, more particularly, Zodiak to the extent possible. Their intention was to kill as many Toufanians as possible from afar with the catapults, and if any one of them was able to ascend closer, then he would be killed by the archers. The cavalry, mostly chariots with sharp blades sticking out of the center of the wheels, was stationed to attack Toufan's warriors if necessary. The infantry moved behind the cavalry to finish the job.

Some hundred thousand soldiers were positioned on the north and south side of the battlefield each to prevent any of the Toufan soldiers from escaping or breaking the surrounding walls of Fars's soldiers. When the navy arrived from behind, they would join them, move forward, and tighten the space in order to assemble them in the middle of the circle, and then the catapults would fire a second round to finish all of them. The Fars army had excelled at this strategy called clipping during many wars and knew exactly how to accomplish it. As for Zodiak, in case he could not be killed, they brought vast nets of knitted iron cables, which were cast by huge torpedoes from afar. Once they threw the iron net over Zodiak, they could close it out and then congest it to get smaller and smaller without having to come within Zodiak's reach. They could then add more layers of iron nets to secure Zodiak's captivity for good.

The navy was proceeding without much resistance, though they demolished everything in their path to prevent any possible ambush from behind.

The king's order to the armed forces was to continue killing enemies until and unless they brought Zodiak to him, dead or alive in captivity. However, the king preferred to see him dead, if possible at all.

The Fars military, the navy included, was notorious for its fast mobility. One of the most effective attributes of the Fars army was to move fast and to act fast. Their equipment and gear were heavy but sat on lubricated wheels, which afforded them to move fast and with ease. They had ball bearings inside the multiple wheels belted together to work as one unit in order to increase speed, maneuverability, and durability in carrying catapults and other heavy equipment. This technology was far ahead of all others, supposedly not yet known by man.

HAGHDAR

The night before the war started, Haghdar and the king reviewed their plans and, despite heavy casualties to the navy, concluded they were on track. The king smiled and said that if they lived through this, he would make the world an even better place for everyone, heaven on earth. Haghdar responded that they would have to go through hell to reach heaven, which was kind of awkward. The king replied that such was life.

"Better get some sleep. Tomorrow is hell day." Haghdar smiled bitterly and went to his sleeping quarters.

Haghdar lay on his bed, trying to sleep, but could not. He could not identify it, but something was not right. He was not particularly worried about the next day. As the king said, other than casualties to the navy, everything was right on schedule. He had victoriously been to many wars with much larger and better trained armies. Fars had sufficient plans and, more importantly, the technology, the likes of which would not be invented for another fifty years, maybe more. Fars was fighting for the good of the god of light and the teachings of the Good Book. Despite all of that, he still felt something was very wrong. Then what was it? He had some strong feeling of anxiety that burned him inside. He thought he was not apprehensive for his own life. He had long before accepted that someday he would pass, either by age, wounds, or another warrior, some young and strong warrior such as himself when he was younger. His purpose was to serve and protect his beloved country under the teachings of the Good Book and did not mind sacrificing his life for it. These mixed and ambiguous feelings kept him awake most of the night. He tossed and turned, trying to find an answer, but none was attained.

The Toufan camp was in disarray. They had to stay at least three kilometers ahead of Fars's navy behind them to avoid their firing. They could see the smoke from the distance and measure the extent of damage and destruction inflicted by Fars's navy. They knew the likelihood of any Toufanian survivor on the path of Fars's navy was extremely slim. However, there was no time for grief since their own lives were in jeopardy. Zodiak knew what expected them ahead. It was going to get much worse once they encountered the Fars army and particularly Haghdar. He rode up and down the line of troops and helped them to carry equipment in order to move faster. It was just that they did not plan for this kind of rush. All their plans were made for the occasion of face-to-face combat with the Fars army. He now realized how technologically advanced Fars was. Even his immortality might not be enough to save Toufan. Above all, he could not allow himself to be captured. In fact, he preferred to be killed rather than be captured alive, but he could not die. Then he thought that death had its reward. Yes, immortality had a price larger than life, a price that he wished he did not have to pay, but it was too late now. He was at the point of no return. He thought his captivity would destroy Toufan forever. Most would be killed, and the rest, if not taken as slaves, would accept Fars as the master for generations. Afterward, there would be only one social class in Toufan. Citizens who were not slaves yet did not have any rights. They would be nomads, empty shells mocked by Fars masters for as long as there was life. These thoughts made him shiver. But then again, he thought, he still had the chance to free his people. His intentions were based on the teachings of the book of the god of light. He had his army, not as large or trained as Fars's but loyal and willing to fight to the end. He must be the source of hope and strength for them. Yes, there was still a chance to win over the agents of the darkness but no room for mistakes.

These conflicting thoughts were eroding his wisdom, and therefore, he must not allow them to distract him. There must be only one thing on his mind—victory. That was all that counted, victory. He pulled himself together and, with a confident voice that shook the mountain, shouted, "Toufanians, stay strong. Victory is ours. Only a few more kilometers and we will show the fate of Toufan's enemies." His tone of voice, self-esteem, and excitement lifted the soldiers' morale. They started moving with exceedingly increasing energy and shouted back, "Victory is ours." Suddenly the Toufan army moved as if they were running to the promised land. They were charged like Zodiak had not seen before.

Zodiak had to move the army as fast as possible for two reasons—first, to stay away from Fars's navy, and second, to reach the Fars army before the Toufanians' morale and confidence subsided.

Alas, moving fast made his warriors tired. Simply, there was not sufficient time to rest. They had to move their equipment with old technology, which in turn slowed them down. Some injured women in the camp, those who participated in liberating their beloved land and fought side by side with the men, needed help often and had to be carried by others. Wounded men had to carry on. There was no help for them. The entire company was doing the best they could. They were working hard.

Zodiak was wary that all this pressure would interfere with the troops' sense of judgment. They might cause mistakes or the inability to carry orders exactly as instructed. The situation was worse than they had predicted and not getting any better. Nonetheless, he noticed the troops were moving faster with confidence and were seemingly ready to go to war with Fars. A frenzied smile briefly appeared on Zodiak's face.

Zodiak ordered those who were sick or could not walk fast enough to be loaded on the carriages to speed up mobility. He was riding up and down the trail, helping anyone needing assistance. Some sick or injured individuals died, but they did not have time to bury them in accordance with the teachings of the book of the god of light. That affected the ethics of the troops, and some wanted to stay behind to bury their corpses. Zodiak calmly explained that although the rituals were required by the old book, there was a good chance that Fars's navy would catch up with them, and considering the circumstances, he could not spare any more lives.

Toufan's army was basically a cavalry. He divided his army into four groups—some ten thousand behind to defend against the Fars navy if and when they caught up with them, some twenty-five thousand to the north, and another twenty-five thousand to the south side of the army to prevent ambush. He rode with the remaining forty thousand soldiers in the middle and front. His plan was to attack the heart of the Fars army, reach the king's camp and kill him, and then kill Haghdar as fast as possible. He had instructed his men to avoid fighting Haghdar and, if confronted with him, to simply run away. Their job was to fight the enemy except for the king and Haghdar. He would take care of them in addition to as many soldiers as he had to kill to get to the king and Haghdar. He told the warriors he did not need any protection or support since he could not be killed, and as the war progressed and the adrenaline pumped into his veins, he would become stronger and faster. In other words, the more he fought, the stronger he became. The only help he needed from his army was in the remote possibility that he was captured, especially at the start of the war when his strength was not fully bloomed. In such case, the army must free him at all costs. He did not think any man-made chain would be strong enough to hold him after a few hours of fighting when his powers exploded, but considering Fars's advanced technology, he did not wish to take any risk.

CHAPTER FORTY-TWO

THE WAR

Early in the morning, just before the sun rose, the Fars army took position in the battlefield. The king had received messages that Toufan's army was within their vicinity. Almost in all major wars, Haghdar rode in front of the cavalry. The Fars tactic was that Haghdar, with Javidan's best warriors following him, would attack the heart of the opposing army to cut through them like a hot knife through butter to reach the camp of the enemy's king. He then would kill the king fast. Once the chain of command was disrupted, the rest of the Fars army would attack and finish the enemy.

That particular morning, Haghdar and Raad were in front line as usual, waiting for arrival of Toufan's army. Haghdar wore full armor. His hood covered his head, face, and neck. He looked like a fierce giant made of iron riding Raad, which was in full armor too. His ensemble made men shake in their boots. He was calm and resolved.

Toufan's army, with Zodiak riding in front, arrived at the battlefield slightly after dawn. The sun was coming up from the east behind the Fars army and directly into their eyes, which made it difficult for them to see Fars army's exact whereabouts. Zodiak looked and immediately saw Haghdar riding Raad in front of the Fars army. The sun shone from the east behind Haghdar, and he could only see his shadow. He was slightly taller and apparently more muscular than

Zodiak. There was no mistake about it. His size, strength, and resolve made Haghdar unmistakably distinctive. In fact, he thought, whatever he had heard about him in the past did not do him justice. He was a monster who could just step on warriors and crush them to the ground. He now knew the reason for the soldiers escaping the battlefield at his sight. He admitted that many, maybe majority of Toufan's army, would be killed by the hands of this monster. Thoughts came to his mind at the speed of light. So this was the agent of darkness who attacked Toufan and took many innocent lives, including the king's and queen Shahrara's, his mother, and attempted to kill him before birth. The only reason Haghdar did not come after him, he reckoned, was because he thought Zodiak was born dead. Otherwise, he would have followed him, found him, and then killed him without any hesitation.

As ruthless as he seemed, Zodiak was to extract his emotionless heart out of his cold body and feed it to the hogs. It was time for this forceful agent of the gods of darkness to go back to the deepest corner of hell. After decades of terror, fear, and crime by the hands of Haghdar, it was time for goodness to prevail.

Toufan's soldiers, on the other hand, were shaken by Haghdar's appearance. Some even knelt in lieu of respect and submission. Not only they were no match for Haghdar and Raad, but the Fars army was enormous. They expanded to where naked eye could no longer see. There were more soldiers and equipment than they could imagine. The speed with which the Fars army positioned or repositioned large troops and gear was beyond their comprehension. Toufanians could not understand how and with what apparatus such speed was possible. It was some kind of a nightmare except it was real. There was no way for Toufan's army to be able to maneuver with that kind of speed. Seeing the Fars army and Haghdar, some soldiers were not sure this was the war for them to partake in. They were not afraid of death but did not wish to die for a lost purpose. They asked themselves what purpose this war could possibly serve if they were all to be killed and Toufan defeated. Some thought maybe they should try to negotiate first. The negotiation might prevent certain death and defeat. Fars might accept a settlement with disadvantageous terms and conditions for Toufan. They most likely would pay higher taxes and lose a portion of Toufan but would retrieve the rest of the country and save many lives. They could hear Fars's drums ordering the cavalry to take position to attack. Worse, Fars's navy was approaching from behind fast. Fars's navy heard the army drumming, signaling the attack, and started drumming too. It seemed like it was the end for Toufan. They were coming to take away their lives, their souls, and everything else they had—the worst kind of death, in total darkness with their greatest fear. Not even the god of light would accept their souls in that state of mind.

The king and Haghdar had orchestrated this war to the perfection—a masterpiece warcraft to be remembered for ages, perhaps forever.

Zodiak recognized the soldiers' change of mood. He had not worn any armor. He did not have any clothes above his waist. His face and upper body were painted with the colors of Seepar to plant the seeds of fear in the heart of the enemy. Seeing signs of fear in the eyes of Toufan soldiers, he immediately jumped and stood on top of the saddle on the back of his horse with one acrobatic move. He lifted his sword in the air and shouted with an assertive voice that shattered the Fars soldiers' poise, "Victory is ours". Reminisce of the time being pursued by Fars's navy. His voice echoed in the battlefield, and Haghdar, the Fars army, and the king of kings heard him. Toufan's warriors heard him loud and clear. Their confidence rose one more time. They lifted their shields and shouted, "Victory is ours. Victory is ours." Zodiak, while standing on the saddle, brought down his sword and, with lightning speed, pushed it through his own heart. The sword broke, but his skin was unaffected—a move no one had seen before, never heard of. The Fars cavalry in the front row who saw the motion shivered. Their horses became restless and started to jump up and down fast. The horses wanted to run away, and the riders could not control them. The frontline cavalry disarranged with disbelief.

Haghdar ordered Raad to take a step forward. Haghdar took a quick glance at the frontline cavalry, a glance that immediately calmed the horses and riders. They then lined up in the ranks again.

Haghdar looked at Zodiak right in the eye from afar, and then Raad stood on its two rear legs. Together they looked like a mountain. Haghdar screamed with a tone that blasted a gust to the face of the opponents. Raad screamed too, which terrified Toufan horses and soldiers.

The king of kings stepped forward and ordered the cavalry to proceed but asked Haghdar to stay with him. He wanted to see what else this warrior was capable of accomplishing. The king told Haghdar that obviously, the rumors they had heard about Zodiak were true. He was big and strong. They could not see his face because it was painted completely, but he was almost Haghdar's size. As a matter of fact, his physique, muscles, and composition resembled Haghdar. He could simply pass for Haghdar if one had not seen either one. The king continued, "This is one warrior who may not be killed, and therefore, only wisdom may defeat him." He might not be killed, but his army would. He would be watching his entire army being killed one by one. The king then said that he was wondering if Zodiak had a heart and, if so, how many deaths of his warriors he could stand before breaking down. He rhetorically stated, "Let us see how many Toufanian lives he can spare."

The Toufan army had no choice but to proceed since Fars's navy was coming from behind, reaching within firing range. The king ordered the cavalry to open up and the huge catapults brought forward. Toufan's army saw them and realized what was coming to them. They started riding, Zodiak in front, toward the Fars army as fast as they could. The king and Haghdar immediately took their position in the heart of Javidan, and the king ordered to fire. Fars drums signaled the navy to fire upon the Toufan army as well. The skies were covered with fire in all directions, and Toufan's warriors fell like leaves in the autumn wind. The king asked Haghdar to engage the war but to avoid Zodiak. He also ordered the best of Javidan to ride with Haghdar to prevent Zodiak from getting close to him. He ordered them not to allow Zodiak to reach within a hundred meters from Haghdar, even at the cost of their lives. He also advised Haghdar not to move in Zodiak's direction toward the center. He must stay on the sides like the rest of the army to avoid being hit by the catapult's fire. He added that they must kill everybody else first. Haghdar engaged, and more of Toufan's warriors were killed. Haghdar was furious and fought like never before. He advanced to the Toufan generals' camp and, in one split second, came face-to-face with the king of Mantik. They saw hatred and despisement in each other's eyes. Haghdar struck him with his sword once and cut him in two.

Zodiak, while fighting against hundreds of Fars soldiers, felt something inside flew away and took to the skies. Deep inside he knew his best friend, the priest from Mantik, was dead at the hands of Haghdar. He was full of rage and anger. He was angry at himself to have forgotten the priest and left him alone. He vowed not to rest until and unless Haghdar was dead.

It was several hours since the war started, and Zodiak had gained full strength. He was unaffected by the catapults' firing and killed two or three Fars soldiers with every strike of his sword. But there were too many of them. He could not see Haghdar or the king of Fars but was on the hunt for them. Zodiak was in the middle and front of his army, fighting. They were surrounded by the Fars army, and the space was getting smaller as the Fars army and navy were tightening the circle.

Fars then brought torpedoes to cast iron nets onto Zodiak. The first iron net landed on Zodiak, and Fars immediately threw another net and then another. Alas, it was too late. He cut through the iron nets like scissors through paper. It only slowed him a little but nothing serious. While Zodiak was breaking free, Fars soldiers tried to put their swords and spears into his heart many times to no avail. Some hit him with their sword on his head to no avail either. They could not pierce his skin nor hurt him. It seemed like he did not lose one gram of energy. In fact, he looked stronger by the minute. Fars lost many soldiers mostly at the hands of Zodiak.

At the end of the day, except for Zodiak, both sides were tired. He wanted to continue until he killed Haghdar, but his top generals suggested rest was needed for the night. Fars had retreated to rest too. Even though Zodiak could fight forever, the soldiers could not, and any attack by him could evoke fighting at night. Considering the size of the Fars army and their equipment and gear, all Toufan warriors could be killed. They already had significant casualties and severe injuries for one day. They needed to stop the fight to allow, at the minimum, the injured to be collected. Zodiak reluctantly accepted for the sake of Toufanians, and the war was postponed until early the next day.

The war continued for seven months. Most Toufan's soldiers were dead by then. In fact, there were less than five thousand soldiers left. Food and water were scarce. They were not able to collect the dead and injured anymore since there were too many of them. Corpses were scattered all around, and vultures came to feed on them. Soldiers were tired, injured, and hungry and illness afloat. The king of Mantik, along with most generals, was dead. The wisdom of the priest was clearly needed as much as fresh and strong warriors. The only person not affected by all of this was Zodiak. He was as strong and determined as ever.

Fars had significant casualties too. They had lost over seven hundred thousand soldiers and marines. Even if Fars won this war, which was not a given by any means, they had major issues to deal with subsequently. Without a strong and effective army, all insignificant rulers and kings would rise against Fars. They had been waiting for this occasion for decades, actually since the start of the Fars dynasty. The king and Haghdar received reports of many rumors going around the country suggesting Haghdar and the king, along with the entire Fars army, were killed in the war against Toufan. Many of the kings' subjects already announced their independence, and some went even further and attacked certain regions of Fars. The country was being broken into small regions. There existed no one pillar to piece the empire together. The court was in no better shape. The king's son was surrounded by adversaries who wanted to establish a council consisting of priests, ministers, and retired generals to govern since the country was in a downward spiral. The prince sent an alarming message to the king, signifying a critical situation and that the king was desperately needed at the throne. However, the situation was grimmer in the battlefield, and he could not leave the war. His wisdom and planning capabilities, in addition to moral support for the troops, were needed more in the battlefield. He was not sure anymore that even Haghdar could win this war. They could fight to the last man. Alas, Zodiak would live and raise another army to rule the Fars empire.

The king had no choice but to find a resolution to this terminating dilemma. There was only one way to settle this grievance. Yes, the severity of the moment left no choice for him but to make the hardest decision. The king cried all night, thinking about unthinkable.

CHAPTER FORTY-THREE

FINAL DECISION

On the night of the last day of the war, the Toufan army was basically annihilated. There survived less than five thousand soldiers, mostly injured, hungry, and sick. Their morale was nonexistent. All top generals and the priest were killed. Zodiak did not have the slightest doubt in his resolve, but his army was practically destroyed. Some high-ranking warriors approached him and requested permission to speak. Zodiak received them inside his quarters. After expressing the customary pleasantries, their captain claimed that the soldiers had lost all hopes. They did not want to continue this war because they knew they would be killed within next few days. They wished for Zodiak to commence negotiations. They believed this was their only chance to perhaps achieve an honorable settlement with Fars even though they suffered material casualties too. Zodiak was against negotiations and wished to continue the war. He said Fars was on the verge of defeat. Some seven hundred thousand soldiers of Fars, the best of their warriors, except Haghdar, were dead. The captain responded that even if that was true, it meant every Toufan soldier killed on an average seven Fars soldiers. They could kill, therefore, another thirty five thousand Fars soldiers before the last of them were killed. Then Zodiak had the entire remaining two hundred and sixty five thousand soldiers, including Haghdar and the king of kings, to himself to kill. The soldiers did not care about what he did after they were dead. Simply put, this was originally a war between Zodiak and Haghdar. True, Haghdar attacked and conquered Toufan. He killed the king and Queen Shahrara. But let us not forget that Fars transformed Toufan from a land of villagers to a technnologically and economically advanced nation. They established law and order, built infrastructures and schools, and created a safe environment for innovation and business. Except for minor violations of citizens' rights, mostly in remote regions, Toufan was flourishing. Toufanians never had so much freedom, security, and wealth. Even during the king's era, the laws were more limiting and the economy primitive. They mostly were at war and fed on other nations' wealth. Fittingly, it was the wish of the remaining soldiers that Zodiak either began negotiations or personally took on Fars. They were through with this war.

Zodiak stayed awake all night, thinking what was to be done. The captain was right. Many lives were lost. Since he took upon himself the venture of finding his father and kill Haghdar, he had killed more men than he could count. In his solitude, he remembered the captain saying this was a war between him and Haghdar. He spoke of the truth. Deep inside he knew this war was not solely to liberate Toufan. He had made a promise to himself, on several different occasions, to kill Haghdar. Even if Fars submitted, he still would kill Haghdar. It was time to put an end to all this killing. If he was determined to kill Haghdar, this was his opportunity. He would then let Toufan govern itself. Yes, he would leave Toufan and go to a faraway place. He would go to a place where nobody knew him and live as an ordinary man, but not before he killed Haghdar. He called upon the captain before dawn and instructed him to go to the Fars camp with a white flag to present his terms to finish this war. He offered to the king of Fars to allow one warrior from each side to fight to the death, and the winner would win the war. This was customary and done in many wars when neither side could defeat the other. He continued that in such case, if Toufan's warrior won, Fars would leave Toufan forever and recognize it as an independent and sovereign country. The two nations would treat each other with respect for eternity. In case Toufan's warrior lost, Toufan would become Fars's ally and pay taxes, but Toufanians must be treated with dignity and the rule of law, equitable to that applied to Far's citizens, must govern the entire country. The captain smiled and said he knew Zodiak would choose the right path.

Affairs were not much better in Fars's camp. The high generals, those who were still alive, requested a meeting with the king of kings and Haghdar. After greetings, the top generals stated that this was an unprecedented situation. Zodiak could not be killed, and that meant he could fight until everybody else was dead. In fact, in all likelihood, that was what he planned. After finishing all, he could raise another army in the next generation or two and conquer Fars without any resistance. All the soldiers would be dead by then, let alone completely depleted Fars's resources. They claimed that even if Fars won this war, the road ahead was long and unpredictable, if not futile. Many kings of different regions had declared their independence. They had raised armies since the beginning of this war. Many of them unified and were aware that not much was left of the Fars's military. They were waiting for the result of this war, and if Fars won, they would start a war of their own against Fars. The soldiers were tired, many injured and sick. More importantly, they had lost all hopes. Soldiers were reluctant to continue the war and expected the king to devise a remedy, one that did not involve them fighting in this war any longer. Some soldiers had already fled the battlefield, and the guards did not stop anyone walking away. Worse, there could be a revolt in the camp, which meant a fight inside the troops. If they continued this war, there was a high possibility that some would join Toufan and Zodiak since they reckoned the odds were more against Fars. The generals continued, with all due respect, it was time to think of Fars's future, whatever was left of it. The king and Haghdar were listening; they knew the generals spoke the truth. The king commanded that they must maintain order at least for another day or two so they could find a solution to the problem. He ordered significant prizes awarded to soldiers to encourage them to continue the war until the king and Haghdar found the answer. The generals declared they would do what they could, nothing short of giving their lives, for their favored king and beloved country but could not give any assurance on behalf of the soldiers. The decision must be made quickly. They expected an answer within next forty-eight hours max.

The king dismissed the generals but asked Haghdar to stay. There was something of extreme importance to discuss.

The king asked Haghdar what he thought of the situation. Haghdar replied that he agreed with the generals. This war could not be led like any other any longer. In fact, they should have thought of other means to conduct this war sometime ago. The king looked at Haghdar in the eyes and said, "Here we are. Everything we worked for and our ancestors worked for is dependent on the decision we have to make now. Nothing else matters at this point." The king noted it was customary during wars like this, when neither side could prevail, to have one warrior from each side to fight, and the winner would win the war. The king started to cry. Haghdar understood his decision before the king could finish his thoughts. Haghdar said he fought one on one against many warriors, including the leader of the barbarians south of the Sea of Fars. He did not have the slightest doubt about this one either and would give his life for his country and his king and best friend, the only family member he had. But this agent of the gods of darkness could not be killed. The king, weeping hardly, said he knew. This fight was not for the great Haghdar to win. This fight was only for gaining some leverage to negotiate reasonable terms with Zodiak before it was over. This was Fars's only chance to settle this war with dignity. Zodiak may not be killed, but Haghdar might not be killed easily either. The Toufanians knew it and therefore would press Zodiak to accept a settlement before the fight concluded. They had to count on the weaknesses of the enemy. That was their only and final chance for an honorable settlement. In fact, if the terms of the settlement were not acceptable to Fars, the war would continue no matter of the outcome. The king put his arms over Haghdar's wide and strong shoulders and wept. Haghdar understood his emotions and thoughts. The king was willing to sacrifice all, including his throne, for the sake of Fars. His own life too. His last duty in life was to obtain a dignified settlement for Fars. He was not to live thereafter. For one last time, they cried together in silence.

CHAPTER FORTY-FOUR

FINALE

The king went to bed with the thought of sending a message to Zodiak the next day early in the morning to offer his terms. He knew the warrior from Toufan, if his offer was accepted, would be Zodiak. He was certain that Zodiak also knew the warrior from Fars would be Haghdar. At times he thought he would volunteer for a one-on-one fight. What was the difference? The Fars warrior would be killed, be it Haghdar or himself. But then again, he had to live to complete the terms of settlement with Toufan. There was no other choice. He was soon after to join his best friend, the larger-than-life Haghdar the great.

The next day, early in the morning, the guards woke up the king to inform him there was a messenger from Toufan. He claimed that he was carrying an urgent message and must see the king without delay. The king thought he most likely had brought the terms for Fars's surrender. Zodiak probably demanded unconditional surrender. He ordered the guards to bring him to his quarters immediately. He also ordered them to ask Haghdar to come to his quarters at once.

The messenger entered the king's quarters. Haghdar entered after him. The messenger rendered greetings and apologized for proceeding with Zodiak's message without further delay. The king listened to the message, paused a second, and told the messenger to go back to Toufan's camp. He would deliberate it with his Generals and send his answer before sunset. The king suggested it would be best, under the circumstances, that both sides refrain from fighting that day so they could peacefully make their decision. The messenger thanked the king and Haghdar and left.

After he left, the king looked at Haghdar. Haghdar knew what he was thinking and promptly said he needed to make preparations for the fight. The king knew there was nothing more to say.

That afternoon the king sent his private messenger to the Toufan camp to declare their acceptance of Zodiak's conditions. The fight was to start in seven days, after they collected the injured and performed the rituals for the dead.

On the eighth day, early in the morning, Haghdar and Zodiak entered the battleground. Haghdar was riding Raad. Zodiak was riding too. Haghdar was in full armor as usual, an iron hood covering his head, face, and neck. Raad was in full armor as well. Zodiak did not wear any clothes from the waist and higher. He had painted his face with colors no one had seen before. Those colors reminded one of darkness, loneliness, and despisement. The clouds started to gather to cover the rising sun. A mild rain started, and the wind started to pick up. The Fars and Toufan soldiers were standing on either side, watching the dreadful fight between the two leaders, each larger than life. The king, sitting on the back of his horse, was watching atop a hill. He thought there would never be another fight like this. Regardless of the outcome, Haghdar and Zodiak's names would go on the pages of history forever. Haghdar, representing Fars, would bring respect and fame to his country for infinity. He admired both warriors but especially Haghdar for what was an apparent suicide for his faith, his country, and his king.

The two warriors fought ferociously all day. Haghdar had struck Zodiak on the head with his mace several times. Those blows would have killed the strongest man or any living for that matter. But Zodiak shook off the blow and became stronger as they fought. At the end of the day, the two warriors went back to their camps to prepare for the fight the next day. Zodiak wanted to fight day and night continuously, but his captain advised him they were negotiating with the king of Fars on the side, and it was best for Toufan to sleep on it for the night.

Haghdar was injured but not to the point incapable of continuing the fight. The king visited him and asked if he was all right. Haghdar answered, "What difference could that make?" They both knew the end result. The king told him negotiations were already on their way, and Fars needed him to extend the fight as long as he could. Haghdar laid down on his bed and closed his eyes.

The next day, early in the morning, both warriors went back to the battleground. They fought all day again and then went back to their camps at sunset. Haghdar's injuries were getting serious, and there was nothing he could do about them. He remembered many fights when he knew he was just toying with his opponent. They simply were no match for him. But now, that feeling of superiority and self-assurance belonged to Zodiak. He knew Haghdar could not kill him. It was just a matter of time before he killed Haghdar.

The king visited Haghdar every night and reported the progress of negotiations. The problem was Zodiak. He believed the terms were already negotiated and there was nothing more to discuss. He would kill Haghdar, and Toufan would be free. Nevertheless, negotiations continued.

As the days passed, the clouds gathered more and more. Dark clouds pushed to each other. The clouds were intensifying by the hour, and the rain and wind became stronger. By the fifth day, hail started, which seemed to get bigger and stronger by the moment. It was difficult for either warrior to walk toward each other because of the heavy wind and rain mixed with hail. The rain, hail, and wind were so intense, it was practically difficult for Haghdar and Zodiak to see each other. The visibility was mired to less than a couple of meters. The black clouds were getting closer to the earth, and the storm slammed their faces.

On the sixth day, Haghdar was badly injured and bleeding heavily. His strength was diminished and confidence vanished. He could hardly lift his sword, let alone strike Zodiak. Raad was also bleeding heavily. It had lost much energy and could hardly carry Haghdar. Its eyes were covered with blood, and its legs lacked strength.

At the end of the sixth day, Haghdar went back to his quarters one last time. He knew the next day was his last. He was bleeding heavily and lost almost all energy and strength. He dropped on the bed and closed his eyes. He knew one day this would come. He was gratified though dyeing in the battlefield and not in bed. The king came to visit him that night. He felt pain in his heart seeing Haghdar in that condition. They did not exchange a word. He just looked at him and left. He thought it would not be long before he joined his best friend. The thought comforted him. Haghdar slowly opened his eyes. He struggled to lift the box his father had given him at his deathbed containing three feathers of Seepar. He remembered what his father told him and decided to seek Seepar's help. It was his last chance, though he was not sure what kind of help Seepar would be able to render him.

He crawled to Raad. Raad had lost blood and energy and was weak too. It knelt to make it easy for Haghdar to get on its back. Haghdar leaned forward and whispered in its ear.

"This would be our last and final mission together. I need you to be quiet and take me to the highest hill behind the Fars army. Nobody should hear or see us leaving or returning." Raad nodded and quietly walked toward the destination. They traveled a long distance where nobody could see them. Haghdar asked Raad to wait for him at the foot of the hill. He stepped down from the saddle and told Raad, "Close your eyes until I come back. This is my last and final order." Raad stood silently without a move. Haghdar walked to the top of the hill, using every bit of energy left in him. The rain stopped despite the clouds becoming more intense and closer to the earth. He took out one of the feathers and lit it. The black clouds condensed and gradually formed a huge, dark, monstrous bird, one which covered the entire sky. Haghdar did not know what was happening. He was somewhat hypnotized. He stared at the clouds until he saw what looked like the large bird, his father, Zesht, had described. Then he heard a deep voice like nothing he had ever heard before.

"What troubles you, my son," said the bird, or that was what Haghdar felt. Haghdar responded that his world and life were in jeopardy. He was fighting the strongest warrior he had seen, whom could not be killed. He needed to salvage his country, his king, and if possible, his life. Seepar said it felt his pain, but no matter what happened the next day, the result would not be what he expected. Haghdar said the situation could not be graver, and he needed to win this fight, even if that meant the end of his life. Seepar said, "There are things worse than death," but if he insisted, Zodiak had one weakness. Seepar continued that it was not sure if Haghdar would want to know about it. Haghdar's heart was enlightened by a ray of hope. He replied that whatever happened the next morning could not be worse than his present situation. He had no choice but to know about Zodiak's weakness. Seepar said Zodiak's left eye was his weakness. Haghdar must shoot him in the left eye. Though first, he must attach the remaining two feathers to the end of his arrow. The feathers would add power, accuracy, and speed to his arrow like nothing he had seen before. He must aim for his left eye and shoot him with every gram of energy he had. The clouds reformed, and Seepar disappeared. Haghdar felt hope, and that gave him some energy. He started crawling back toward Raad, noticing it was watching the saga. Haghdar said it should not have watched him. This was one journey he must take alone. Raad shook its head, meaning it would not leave Haghdar. Haghdar said it was making a mistake. Its life must continue even if his would not. And that was an order. Raad looked straight into his eyes. Haghdar understood. They were one. Raad wanted life with him. They lived or died together. Haghdar did not say another word. They quietly walked back to the Fars camp.

The storm started to rise wildly. Heavy rain, wind, and hail started once again, and the dark clouds intensified. The black clouds were close to the earth, curtailing vision. Nobody, whether in the Fars or Toufan camp, was able to sleep that night. A heavy storm, the likes of which no one had ever seen before, would not let them. Many warriors believed the next morning was going to be the end of time and the end of the world. They prayed all night, pleading to the god of light to have mercy on their souls and accept them after life.

Haghdar woke up earlier than usual the next day. It was still dark, and he lit a lamp. The wild storm persisted all night. Yet it was getting stronger. Haghdar felt anger and resentment in the storm.

There was nothing ordinary about this weather, this fight, and this opponent. He still felt something was dramatically wrong but was not able to figure it out. It was a discomforting feeling. He tried to rid himself of it and concentrate on the matter at hand. He then carefully installed the two feathers at the end of his best arrow and checked his bow. The rod on his bow was so strong, no man could pull it. He then started to wear his armor, getting ready for the final confrontation.

The Fars army had watched the fight during the last six days and knew about Haghdar's condition. They were preparing to leave Toufan forever. They did not expect the fight to last long that day. It could be only minutes before Zodiak finished Haghdar. Some had thought Haghdar might have died of severe injuries the night before.

To their surprise, Haghdar entered the battleground riding Raad. They both looked resolved and strong. The Fars soldiers knelt and dropped their heads. It was another proof that Haghdar was beyond an ordinary man. The king of kings was watching from afar with a glare of hope in his eyes, seeing Haghdar. Haghdar was back, and the king could feel confidence in his eyes under his iron hood. Zodiak was waiting for him. He had decided to finish him quickly and to put him out of his misery immediately.

The storm was getting stronger. It was so strong, it did not allow much movement. The warriors could not see each other, and the storm precluded them from moving toward each other. Both warriors' horses were struggling to take a step forward. The clouds were more than black. They had colors of the deepest corner of the darkness. Deep and dark purple mingled with charred bloodstain.

The soldiers on both sides took cover. They thought it was the end of time and the end of their day. Raad took one step forward, and so did Zodiak's horse. In one split second, Haghdar saw Zodiak's face painted heavily. He lifted his bow and held the arrow between his three fingers. He pulled the rod with all his strength.

The clouds collided, creating thunder with a deafening sound. Black clouds were close to the surface, surrounding the soldiers and thereupon hindering their vision. They could not see anything. The king was on his horse's back on top of a hill. He could not see either

Haghdar or Zodiak. But he could see the clouds shaping in the form of a disgusting colorful monster. The colors were more than frightening. They were threatening. He thought this was beyond a simple fight. This was an eternal war between the gods. He was scared just like everybody else but could not close his eyes. He was determined to see the fight through. Deep inside he had a feeling that all of this might not be for nothing. He had to understand its purpose.

Haghdar aimed at Zodiak's left eye and released the arrow with all his strength. Zodiak was still pushing forward to reach Haghdar when the arrow, with the speed of light and the power of a thousand lightning bolts, pierced his left eye. In a matter of less than a second, he fell to the ground, rolling in his blood. He could not imagine how this could be possible. Maybe the magic was over. The storm was getting stronger and stronger. The clouds intensified even more, if that was possible, and shaped up like a solid monstrous bird. Haghdar finally reached Zodiak's body. He sat on Zodiak's chest and removed his hood. He looked into Zodiak's eye and, for a second, saw a familiar glare, somehow similar to his own. For a split second, he had the same feelings he had before the start of the war. Once again, he felt this was not right.

Haghdar asked Zodiak for the name. He replied Zodiak. He then asked him for the name of his father. Zodiak could hardly speak. So with a weak tone, answered he was not sure. Haghdar asked if he knew his mother's name. Zodiak, with his last breath, said Shahrara, queen of Toufan. Suddenly, everything was so clear to Haghdar. It was like all the spotlights in his mind were turned on and connected spontaneously. He looked above. Zodiak was looking above in the same direction. They both saw Seepar. Raad was watching too. Only they knew what that was. The storm had gathered immense power. Haghdar, staring at Seepar above his head, screamed so loud that the entire battlefield shook. Raad was looking at Seepar as well. It immediately jumped toward Haghdar to help him. In a nanosecond, Seepar clapped its dark wings together, creating lightning that brightened the entire sky. The light was so bright, it blinded all for a second. As Raad reached Haghdar to save him, the lightning split into three branches. One hit Raad, one hit Haghdar, and the third at the end of the arrow stuck in Zodiak's left eye and then went through his eye and skull. The lightning burned all three of them into ashes simultaneously. The strong wind scattered their ashes, and rain and hail washed them away before anybody could see the occurrence. They disappeared as if they never existed. Then the clouds dispersed, and the sun shone on both camps.

The lightning had blinded the king like all others momentarily. He did not see the incident but was the only person who understood the purpose of all of this. He dropped his head and prayed to the god of light to accept their souls for showing the humans the way in life and with their death.

He then heard a deep voice inside or he thought he did, a voice which would make a man tremble. "War is not the answer. Peace and tolerance is the only path to beings' prosperity, the one and only path."

The End

About the Author

Writing for the author is a way to relay to the readers his imagination, desires and ideas, all of which is normally kept with utmost privacy in today's world, in an adventurous context. With artificial intelligence increasingly running our lives, he hopes that *Haghdar The Great Story* touches and arouses the readers' deepest feelings and emotions while creating excitement.

Haghdar, the Great Story will help readers leave everyday life's complications and travel to faraway places full of mystery yet somehow relevant to their lives.

The author received his MBA from Minnesota State University, Mankato. During his undergraduate studies, he took two years of psychology and sociology, which were utilized extensively in various parts of the book. He has written poetry and short stories, but this is his first published book. He also writes music and plays drums as a hobby. Some of the music he has written with his son (a music instructor) are available on YouTube. The name of the band is H2SKETCH.

The author has lived in Southern California since 1984 and has three sons.

CPSIA information can be obtained
at www.ICGtesting.com
Printed in the USA
BVHW031432091219
566104BV00001B/57/P